The Island Man

& other stories

PHILIP CUNNINGHAM

GUILDHALL PRESS

D1494233

Published in December 2014

Guildhall Press
Unit 15, Ráth Mór Business Park
Bligh's Lane
Derry
Ireland
BT48 0LZ
(028) 7136 4413
info@ghpress.com
www.ghpress.com

Guildhall Press gratefully acknowledges the financial support of the
Arts Council of Northern Ireland as a principal funder under its Annual
Funding Programme.

The author asserts his moral rights in this work in accordance with the
Copyright, Designs and Patents Act 1998.

Cover image © Philip Cunningham

A CIP record for this book is available from the British Library.

Acknowledgements

This personal collection of short stories, poetry, mini-sketches and nostalgic references would not have been possible without the generous funding support received from the NI Arts Council under their Individual Artists programme. Therefore, many thanks to Damian Smyth and Julie McBride for their belief, and the courtesy, patience and assistance afforded me throughout the administrative process.

I would like to acknowledge the ongoing interest shown and unstinting support offered by fellow writers – and friends – Garbhan Downey and Dave Duggan. Thanks to Patricia McAdams of the Central Library, facilitator of the successful Creative Writers Group in which I had the pleasure of participating for a number of years and where I began honing my writing skills. Acknowledgements are also due to the friendly and skilled Guildhall Press staff for their help and advice: Joe McAllister, Kevin Hippsley, Declan Carlin, Jenni Doherty, Peter McCartney and Paul Hippsley.

I owe a very special thanks to my wife, Rosita, who patiently read and corrected much of my work, which has undoubtedly helped to create a more entertaining read.

I must also take this opportunity to mention the sad passing of our valued friend Mickey McGuinness at the beginning of 2014. Mickey was a very knowledgeable local historian and dedicated member of the Guildhall Press board as well as being a frequent contributor to the Guildhall Press output over many years. With his friendly smile and delightful tales, Mickey brought so much pleasure to everyone he came into contact with in Derry and beyond.

I hope you will find much enjoyment in exploring my book wherein its pages you will encounter humorous situations, romance, talking rebellious babies, boys playing truant, an island man and many other dubious and interesting characters from all walks of life. Happy reading.

I wish to dedicate this book to my late sister Susie (June 1936 to October 2014). Susie was an avid reader and used the services of the Derry City Central Library every week. She was especially keen on Irish short stories and was eagerly looking forward to reading this book, always asking when it would be published. But, alas, Susie left her own large family, husband Eamonn and us, her brothers and sisters, much too soon, leaving a huge void in all of our lives.

Susan

By Joanne Coyle, Grange, Burt, County Donegal

I carry her photo in my mind
Her face a place to rewind my memories to find
My sister still, Susan, a grown-up and a girl
I talk to her on my travels, hear her unassuming tone
when I'm alone
I see her sparkle on the shore, in the water as white
feathers on a swan
I hold her hand in the sand
Keep her close with my camera, a nostalgic necklace,
my childhood chain linked with love
When day is dusk and the evening ends, I will walk her
home to my heartstrings where she can stay and play

Contents

Rose Cottage

Harry McCay and his wife Molly worked together in Tillie's shirt-manufacturing factory in Derry until they were offered early retirement, he at sixty and Molly at fifty-five. After much thought and discussion, they took up the offer and resigned themselves to the fact that getting older was just one of the inescapable phases of life. They had two children, Stephen and Emma, now grown-up and married and living in the city.

It wasn't too long after retiring that Molly unfortunately passed away and Harry's whole zest and reason for living were shattered. Here he was now, living alone with only his memories and a broken heart in a big empty house. Stephen and Emma eventually persuaded him to sell up and move to County Donegal – where Molly had always wished to spend the rest of her days.

He heeded their suggestions and rented a small holiday cottage on a five-year lease just a few miles from Derry on the shores of Inch Lake in County Donegal. Over time, he planned to buy the cottage outright for his family's use. In the meantime, he would hide his feelings of loss from them.

'Rose Cottage' was the name on the gate, which was framed by a wooden trellis arch entwined with climbing roses. The small front garden was carpeted with a neat lawn bordered by a bed of small flowering plants that displayed a profusion of colour throughout the spring and summer months. At the rear was a slightly larger garden surrounded with a fuchsia hedge and sown out in small quantities of table vegetables, herbs and a few drills of potatoes.

Two years went by and the gardens were transformed to his satisfaction. It was there that Harry spent most of his daylight hours, pottering about, his only wish being that his wife could have been there to enjoy what she had always dreamed about. Only a few of his neighbours stopped briefly to speak to him when he was in the front garden. One old man who frequently passed his gate always stopped for a few minutes to peer into the garden and to look stony faced at the front of the cottage, never once acknowledging Harry's greetings. *What a grumpy, nosey old skitter,* thought Harry. *That old boy seems to resent my presence here, but he can go jump in the lake.*

Thoughts of his dear Molly were always uppermost in Harry's mind and he began to feel as though she were there beside him in the garden. In the evenings as he rested on the wooden seat at the front of the cottage overlooking the lake, he could feel Molly sitting beside him and would often say, 'You know, Molly, we must be the happiest couple in Ireland, living here amidst all this quiet beauty and listening to the birdsongs from morning to night.' He imagined he could feel Molly holding his hand to show him that she was happy and at ease.

In springtime, the countryside would come alive again. The parent swans would accompany their little dark cygnets as they dipped their long necks into the waters to feed on the vegetation growing in the shallows.

Other water birds – coots, grebes and mallard ducks – could also be seen escorting their newly fledged broods along the edges of the reeds, teaching them how to fend for themselves.

Four and a half years had now gone by and Harry was well settled in; it was as though he had lived there for most of his life. He knew that Molly had taken her place alongside him and could feel her presence accompanying him wherever he went. His family visited him often and Harry told them that he felt very content knowing that their mother was always near at hand. Stephen and Emma were happy to agree with him, knowing it was a part of the healing process.

One warm, dry September evening, Harry was busy tidying up the vegetable garden. On putting the garden tools back into the shed, he noticed something inside an empty flowerpot that lay on its side underneath the workbench. He frowned questioningly as he reached for it. *How in thunder did this wallet come to be lodged inside this pot?* he thought to himself. *It must have been lying inside there for a long time, judging by its dusty, perished-looking state.* Opening it gently in case it would disintegrate in his fingers, he carefully examined its contents: a holy medal of Our Lady with its string still attached, a small brass key and two slightly faded photographs.

Harry called on Molly to come and have a look at what he had found. He examined the pictures. One was of a young man and an elderly woman standing in front of a cottage, not unlike the one he was now living in. The other picture was of the same man and three children standing beside a young woman seated in a wheelchair, also taken in the front garden of the same cottage. He turned the photographs over and could just barely read some faded lettering. Squinting his eyes, he was able to make out what they said: John Convery with his mother, Jane, at Inch Cottage, September 1940.

The other picture had somewhat similar handwriting on it: John and Mary Convery with Noel, Nora and Seán at Inch Cottage, September 1940.

He looked carefully at each picture again. 'Mmm, this must have been his mother and his wife and children,' he said aloud. 'So, the cottage was originally called Inch Cottage. I imagine that the new owners, or whoever put that rose-lattice arch over the garden gate, renamed it.'

He turned the pictures over again to examine the people in more detail. 'Isn't that a very strange coincidence, Molly?' he said. 'These photos were taken in the front garden of this cottage about sixty years ago in 1940 when the children were about ten or eleven years of age; that would put them in their seventies if they haven't died by now.'

He looked carefully at the pictures again and, holding up the medal, exclaimed, 'This is the same medal that the elderly woman is wearing around her neck in that photograph.'

He lifted out the casket key. 'Do you know what, Molly? I'll bet this is the key of that little decorative metal box that I found under that wardrobe in the front bedroom last year.'

He closed the wallet, put it into his back pocket and returned to his chores. He became so engrossed in his work he forgot about the brass key.

Next morning, Harry was up bright and early and Highland Radio was emitting its usual Country and Westerns. As he sat enjoying his breakfast, he heard a vehicle stopping at the front gate. He went out to meet the postman and, after their usual 'good morning' exchanges, he returned with a brown envelope.

Harry slit the envelope open and read its contents. It was a letter from the estate agent telling him that his five-year lease would be up in another few months and that he should look for other accommodation. The cottage was to be demolished to make way for the construction of a two-storey house that would be sold on the market.

His jaw dropped; he was stunned. 'What will we do, Molly? We are going to lose our home and there is nothing I can do about it. I'll have to contact Stephen and Emma as soon as possible.'

That evening, Harry was still in shock as he half-heartedly pottered about in the front garden, going through the motions, picking out a weed here and there. As he shuffled about, he became aware of somebody watching him from the gate. It was the old stony-faced man from up the road.

Harry greeted him. 'Hello.'

'Hello,' the man replied, making Harry freeze to the spot. This was the first time that he had spoken. The old man spoke again, bringing Harry to his senses.

'I hear you got notice to quit.'

Harry paused before replying, 'That's right. I was informed by letter from the agent this morning. But how did you know?'

The old man shifted his cap before answering. 'Word gets around these places faster than you think. You see, the people who rent out that cottage live on the other side of the island.'

They conversed for quite a while and Harry learned that the old man was called Seán Convery, the youngest of the three children who had once lived in the cottage in the 1940s along with their parents and grandmother, who owned the cottage. She died in 1943 and Seán's mother, who was in poor health, passed away the following year. His father, unable to cope with the loss, sank into depression, neglected the family and eventually went into hospital. The three children were put into an orphanage and it was when they were living there that their father died of a broken heart. They were then fostered out to different families in the south of Ireland. Seán, the only one left of his family, came back again to Donegal when he was nineteen and worked on a farm. Eventually, he married and came back again to live with his wife in a cottage just up the road. They had no family and his wife never ventured too far from her hearth.

Harry inquired, 'Why did you not move back again into the cottage that was once your home?'

Seán thought for a few moments and chose his words carefully.

'When the cottage lay empty for a while and people learned that my father had passed away and that we were scattered, a man called John Hogan from the other side of the island moved into it. He was the father of James Hogan, who claims to own it now. Also, the deeds of the cottage were lost even before my father died in hospital. So you see, no-one has any documents to prove that the cottage rightly belongs to me.'

Harry invited him in, whereupon Seán looked about him and remarked on the improvements that had been made since he and his family had happily lived there over sixty years before.

Harry made a cup of tea and they talked for a bit before he remembered the old wallet he had found in the shed. He showed the contents to Seán, whose eyes filled up as he gazed at the pictures. He remembered the holy medal that always hung about his grandmother's neck.

He handed the pictures back to Harry, who said, 'These pictures and the wallet belong to you, Seán, and I also have something else belonging to you that I found in the house.'

Harry fetched the box from the front bedroom and placed it on the table in front of Seán. 'I found this under the wardrobe last year and had forgotten all about it until I found that key in the wallet yesterday.'

Seán, his hands now shaking, opened the box and lifted out some yellowed papers. Among them were his and his brother and sister's birth certificates and his parents' marriage certificate. One of the most important pieces turned out to be the deeds of Inch Cottage.

After the excitement had subsided, Seán and Harry discussed the implications of the precious find. Eventually, Seán thanked Harry and left to arrange to bring the matter to the attention of a law firm in order to restore legal ownership of the cottage to its rightful owner, which was, of course, himself, being the only surviving heir.

From their meeting that day, Harry and Seán became close friends. He was allowed to stay in Rose Cottage for a nominal rent for as long as he wished.

Not long after the agreement had been settled, Harry's mind was more at ease, knowing that Molly had somehow been responsible for guiding him to the lost wallet. He no longer spoke outwardly to Molly but lovingly felt her there always in his heart at Rose Cottage.

Bad Blood

RUC District Inspector Paddy McCloskey was an overbearing, pompous brute of a man. Standing 6ft 4ins and heavily built with a roaring voice, he was nicknamed 'the Bull'.

On 4 March 1957, he left his own station in Omagh on a very important visit to the barracks in Strabane, where Sergeant Samuel Ross was in charge. Ross had assembled eight of his best men in the operations room, having being notified in advance of the District Inspector's visit. McCloskey, grim faced and angry, made his entry by violently pushing open the operations room door, causing it to slam noisily against the wall.

There was an uneasy silence in the room, some of the men fidgeting with their pencils and notepads or adjusting their tunics as they sat looking straight ahead. They all knew what to expect from the Bull, especially in the knowledge that the IRA had carried out a successful operation on both sides of the Irish border earlier the previous morning – and, to make things worse, daring to make fools of the RUC inside their own jurisdiction. Now McCloskey stood glowering over them, wanting one, just one, of them to give him an excuse to vent his anger on the whole cowering lot. He waited a long three minutes, searching their faces before he let off a stream of curses about the IRA and the lily-livered, lazy, incompetent men now seated in front of him in the Strabane Barracks.

'I'm sure you have all been briefed about the hijacking of the Derry train yesterday morning at St Johnston,' he scowled. 'Or were you more concerned about booking drunkards and checking out faulty bicycle lamps instead of keeping your bloody eyes and ears open for information about those dirty, murdering thugs who ran the goods train into the GNR station on the Foyle Road?' He paused to move his eyes around their sombre faces. 'And it all happened under your bloody useless noses,' he roared, roughly pounding the brass tip of his hawthorn cane on the wooden floor.

The *Derry Journal* had carried the full story on its front page that morning with a picture of the demolished buffers and platform, the wrecked engine and carriages pointing towards the roof of the station.

At five o'clock in the morning of 3 March 1957, shortly after leaving Strabane station, four masked men at St Johnston hijacked the goods train with its eleven fully loaded wagons. It continued to the small stop of Porthall on the edge of the River Foyle, where they forced the driver to stop the train. They then ordered the engine driver, the fireman and the two guards to get off, telling the four to walk back along the line to Strabane. Three of the IRA men also alighted from the train and left the scene, leaving their one remaining colleague on the train. He then proceeded to drive it away and as it neared the Derry station, he increased the train's speed before jumping off. Luckily, no casualties occurred during the incident.

All remained silent as DI McCloskey moved towards the operations map on the wall, crisply slapping it with his stick and resting the tip at a point on the map. He went on to tell them about receiving reliable information about another intended attack by the IRA on the small border Customs post at Urney, a short distance from Strabane. The attack was planned to take place that evening at dusk. He wore an angry expression as he spoke sternly.

'In the interests of your own safety, and that of my informer, I want each of you to take heed of every single word of the plan that I am about to unfold to save the post and its officers.'

After laying out his plan, he quietly threatened the men.

'I warn you all now, if there is even one small hitch during this operation, I will personally see that some of you will be dismissed from the force. I want these cowardly snakes all either dead or captured. Do you all understand?' he roared. 'Not one of them is to escape, even if you have to put your own selves in the firing line. I want the officers under my command to be the ones to take the honours for putting an end to the IRA's murderous border campaign once and for all.'

DI McCloskey himself would co-ordinate the ambush from the barracks. Four other more experienced men from the Omagh Barracks would join Sergeant Ross and his men and all would be lying in wait for the IRA men as they approached across the border. 'Sergeant Ross will be in constant contact with me here in the operations room by walkie-talkie at all times,' he finally added.

Sergeant Ross dismissed his men before discussing the current affairs of the barracks and district operations with McCloskey.

Inspector McCloskey was always more cautious when he was alone with Sergeant Ross, whom he had good reason to be more wary of than any other member of the force. He believed that Sergeant Ross had attempted to discredit him in the past and that he was a scheming, ambitious man who had risen to his present position by devious means since joining the RUC only three years before. 'A very dangerous and power-hungry man,' was how one of McCloskey's close associates had described him.

Ross knew McCloskey's family background extremely well, having grown up in the same area of County Tyrone himself. He knew that McCloskey's father, Seán, had owned a pub and was very sympathetic towards the old IRA during the 1916 Easter Rising. He had even disinherited Patrick for joining the RUC. Ross also knew that the only other son, Dan McCloskey, younger than Patrick by five years, was a known Republican sympathiser and had been questioned a few times about his acquaintances. Dan had inherited the public house after the death of his parents and had sold up the business and gone to live in County Monaghan with his wife and family. Indeed, Sergeant Ross knew the McCloskey family history exceptionally well.

***

That evening, Sergeant Ross took his officers to Urney, where he positioned himself and all but two of his men on both sides of the approach road leading from the bridge at the River Finn to the British Customs border post, the IRA's intended target. The other two officers went inside the Customs hut to await the intended attack. Before long, a car carrying four IRA men pulled up near the post. Three men emerged carrying guns and a canvas sack that held a bomb. They swiftly approached the post and were about to burst through the front door when the waiting RUC men opened fire from inside. The leading IRA man fell instantly as a bullet caught him in the chest. The other two retreated to the car and it was then that Sergeant Ross fired a shot in their direction, hitting one of them in the thigh. That was the signal to his men hiding on both sides of the road to open fire on the car and the two IRA men on the road, one of whom was now getting back into the car. A hail of bullets entered his back and he fell face-first onto the road. The wounded IRA man was also shot dead as the car began to take off. It managed to travel just fifty yards before it swerved and crashed through a wire fence to end up on its roof in a field, all the while being fired at by the RUC ambushers who had followed it on foot. The driver was found slumped over the steering wheel. He was dragged from the car and laid out flat on the road, still alive but bleeding profusely from his legs.

The operation was extremely successful: three senior IRA men killed and the remaining one, the car driver, seriously wounded.

District Inspector McCloskey showed no emotion that evening as he stood in the operations room, tapping his stick against the palm of his hand while Sergeant Ross triumphantly led his men in for debriefing. Their jubilation was obvious from the excited chatter among them, the presence of the Bull not registering any fear or unease among them now.

Sergeant Ross was smiling and unable to hide his pride as he stood alongside Inspector McCloskey, thinking, *This evening of glory will take me further on the road to my promotion.* He placed a heavily laden green canvas sack on the table in front of DI McCloskey, who welcomed the men, congratulating them on their excellent evening's work. He aimed his comments towards the policemen only, deliberately excluding Sergeant Ross. The sergeant clenched his fists and narrowed his eyes with painful annoyance at the inspector's intended snub in front of all his men. *The big, ignorant gobshite will be sorry he did that sooner than he thinks,* he thought.

Sergeant Ross then congratulated his men and gave a brief description of the ambushing of the IRA unit's car.

'The IRA men had a bomb with them and they intended to blow up the Customs post. It has been taken away to be safely detonated, as it was found to be unstable,' he said.

Ross then began to take the contents out of the sack and laid them on the table: one Thompson sub-machine gun, one rifle, two handguns and a number of British Army WWII hand grenades. He tidied them neatly side by side before reaching into the sack again. *Now we'll really see what the Bull is made of,* he thought. And, with a huge grin, he took a blood-stained brown boot from the sack while looking at McCloskey to see how he would react. Inspector McCloskey's eyes opened wide and he let out a gasp.

'Where did this come from?' he asked in astonishment.

Ross smiled as he answered sarcastically. 'So you recognise it, then, *Mr* Paddy McCloskey? Do you see the little Tricolour tab stitched onto the side of the boot?' He held it up in front of Inspector McCloskey's face. 'Aren't these the only kind of boots your brother Dan was ever known to wear?'

Sergeant Ross was enjoying his moment with the Bull McCloskey. Now he was getting revenge for being humiliated and for all the other times that the Bull had browbeaten him in front of his own men. He also believed that Inspector McCloskey would surely be discredited and forced to leave the RUC because of his brother's involvement in the attempted attack on the Customs post.

District Inspector McCloskey's face went pale. His voice was more subdued and timid now as he spoke.

'So my brother Dan was one of the casualties? Did he say anything before he died?'

Ross was enjoying inflicting the pain on McCloskey and took a few seconds to choose his words before replying.

'Unfortunately, your scum of a brother didn't die. We shot both his legs off and he is now under guard in the Omagh hospital.' Ross paused for another few seconds to let his words sink in before continuing, 'He did speak, though, before he went unconscious. The sentimental fool told me to look in the boot of his car and find a metal cash box with your name on it and to give it to you.'

Sergeant Ross took the box from the sack and laid it gently on the table. 'I believe this belongs to you, Mr Paddy The Bull McCloskey,' he announced with venom.

McCloskey winced and put his hand tenderly on the box that he hadn't seen since he and Dan were boys. The name Paddy McCloskey was written with faded white paint on the lid. It was the metal cash box that his father had given to him in his innocent childhood days. He recalled having locked many of his secret possessions in it: marbles, sports medals, penknife, coins and other such precious things that boys treasured then. He also remembered the day he turned sixteen, the day he passed the box on to Dan. *I can still see the delight on his face when he held the treasured box close to his chest all those years ago,* he thought. He remembered, too, the day he announced to his parents that he had joined the RUC and how his father didn't speak but turned his back on him before walking from the house and out of his life for good.

Sergeant Ross, now wearing a grin, broke the silence, saying, 'You can open it in the privacy of my office if you wish, Inspector, just in case there might be something personal belonging to you inside it, like a yoyo, or maybe a toy gun.'

Inspector McCloskey glowered at him and retorted, 'I wasn't intending to open it here in front of you and those gloating fools sitting there anyway.' With trembling hands, he lifted the box and went stomping into Ross's office, slamming the door behind him.

DI McCloskey, now alone, set the box down on a thick, heavy desk. He tenderly placed the palms of his huge hands on the lid and gently moved them over and around its sides as he remembered the joy he had felt when his father had first given it to him. It was secured with a barrel-combination lock; only his father, himself and Dan knew the correct code sequence to open it. He nervously fumbled with the lock for a few seconds as he recalled the six numbers. Inspector Patrick McCloskey, not so much the Bull now but a quivering child, began whispering, 'Nine, eight, one, nine, one, six,' as he slowly turned the chambers in sequence.

Gently, he raised the lid and was instantly blown across the room by the deadly explosion.

***

The next morning's *Strabane Herald* carried the full story of the successful ambush on the front page, ending with an account of the fateful blast in the Strabane Barracks.

The booby-trap bomb killed courageous District Inspector Patrick McCloskey and slightly injured five of his loyal RUC comrades who were also present in the barracks. Sergeant Samuel Ross, who had been in charge of the injured constables, was miraculously uninjured.

Meeting Liam Neeson

Mary Campbell from Derry's Lecky Road was just past eighteen and had recently begun her first year at Queen's University in Belfast and she loved it. She soon made friends with a couple of other girls her own age from Omagh and Dungiven who shared the same rented house in the Holy Land district. That was the most popular place for students of every age, creed and nationality to reside. 'An exciting, colourful and wonderful experience,' was how Mary described it to her two sisters when she returned home every weekend. She told them great stories about the many famous personalities who regularly frequented Belfast's shops and nightspots.

Mary shared one particular story with them as they sat in their front room on a wet Saturday evening. It was about the time she and her two friends Linda and Siobhan met Liam Neeson, the famous actor from Ballymena, while strolling through Botanic Gardens one evening. He was relaxing and enjoying the sunshine and Mary recognised him first. 'Hello, Mr Neeson,' she said.

Liam responded in his Irish-American accent. 'Hi, girls, have a seat. I've being hoping to speak to some lovely Belfast ladies since I arrived yesterday.'

The girls knew that he was in town making a film and didn't put him off his notion that they were three Belfast girls.

Mary's sisters listened with excitement and slight envy as she related every word of their conversation with Liam Neeson.

'He especially loved my accent. He said it sounded very nice and that he would love to meet my mother. He also told us that he would like to bring us over to the USA when we finished our studies at the end of the year.'

What she didn't tell them about was an incident that occurred the following Monday evening when she and her housemates went to the launderette near the Holy Land. The three of them were watching their clothes tumbling about and eyeing up a couple of male students sorting out their dirty laundry when they saw Liam enter, all 6ft-4ins of him, drawing admiring squeaks from Mary and her companions. He carried a cream-coloured cloth shopping bag with the initials LN on it and sat down next to the girls, causing them to turn their faces away from him in case he would recognise them.

'Holy Mother of God! Look at the state of the three of us with no make-up on. I hope he doesn't see us,' Mary whispered as she glanced sideways at him. They peeked at him putting his laundry into one of the machines.

He sat down, began browsing through a magazine and, with the tail of his eye, caught Mary looking at him. Lowering the magazine, he said, 'Hello, do I know you?'

Linda and Siobhan got up and went to their machines to escape his attention, leaving red-faced Mary to her fate.

'No, I don't think so,' she answered, 'although I think I know who you are by the initials on your laundry bag.'

He smiled without another word and resumed reading his magazine.

The other two, relieved that he hadn't noticed them, came back and sat beside Mary again to watch his laundry tumbling about in the machine. Red boxer shorts, blue boxers, a white something with red and blue stripes, silky pink things and an assortment of shirts and socks. A few items that drew most of their attention looked like ladies' pink and white undergarments tangled through the rest of the wash. Their own washing had finished and been tumble-dried and they removed and carefully folded each fresh-smelling piece. He watched them while his clothes were now drying. 'I wish I were as neat with my washing as you girls,' he remarked as his machine came to a stop.

Mary asked if he needed some help to take out his clothes and fold them. *His accent is more like a Ballymena person's now,* she thought. *He probably wants to blend in more with his kinfolk.* She made a funny face at her watching companions as she helped him to retrieve his laundry. While she was folding a shirt, she timidly said, 'I never expected someone like you to have to do his own laundry. Like, I thought that you just bought new clothes when your others got dirty.'

He laughed. 'I'm not that extravagant, you know,' he said in his best Ballymena voice. 'It's the way me ma reared me, to be thrifty.'

Linda and Siobhan stood back a bit, watching and listening with amused smiles on their faces. 'You know something?' Linda whispered enviously. 'I think Liam has a bit of a crush on Mary and I wouldn't like to be her if his wife gets to find out about it. You know the way them big shots are always running to lawyers at the least thing.'

Mary neatly folded all his laundry, including boxers, ladies' undies, socks and LN-initialled handkerchiefs and carefully placed them into his cream bag.

'There you are, sir. How's that for service?'

He leaned towards her and pecked her on the cheek.

'You're a wee dote, thanks. And if I weren't already married, I would ask you and your friends out for a night.' He looked towards them and winked. 'I hope to meet you three lovely ladies again,' he said and left them standing starry-eyed and sighing.

Mary just couldn't dare tell her sisters a word about everything that happened that Monday evening in a Belfast launderette. She would have been mortified if they ever found out about her seeing a piece of paper falling from the Ballymena man's pocket as he went out of the launderette and the three of them running after him with the folded paper. They caught up with him before he entered a confectioner's shop next door.

'This here receipt or note dropped out of your pocket,' they said in unison.

He smiled. 'That's very kind of you, girls, but I would have thrown it in the waste paper bin anyway.'

'We thought it might have been something of importance,' said Mary with a twinkle in her eye.

'Nothing of any value but my name on the back of it,' he assured her. 'There must be more than one Lesley Nixon in this country and I also have a few relatives back in Ballymena called that as well.'

The three girls stood wide-eyed and open-mouthed with shock.

'Cheerio, and thanks again for your help,' said Lesley as he turned on his heels and went into the sweet shop.

It didn't take many minutes for them to figure out that

Lesley Nixon wasn't the same person they'd met a few days before in Botanic Gardens.

'If it wasn't for us finding that receipt, we would have been some fools telling everybody at home that we helped Liam Neeson to do his laundry,' said Siobhan.

'I knew there was something different about him, the way he talked and all, and the way he didn't even recognise us,' said Mary.

Her companion Linda teased her. 'Sure you were all over him, Mary, and you couldn't fold his drawers quickly enough when he asked you.'

'Well, even so,' said Siobhan, 'we can always say that we met the real Liam Neeson in Botanic Gardens and then did his stand-in's washing in a Belfast launderette.'

Mary's cheeks went red, saying, 'Don't you two ever breathe a word about that Lesley Nixon character to a living soul or I will never speak to you ever again.'

And with that, the three friends swore a vow of secrecy and laughed their way home to the Holy Land to continue their exciting adventure of university life.

The Nudist Painter

It is a Sunday evening and Wullie and Cissy Daly are in the kitchen. Wullie is sitting at the table reading a newspaper and Cissy is washing up the dinner dishes at the sink. There is an uneasy quietness after the row that Cissy had kicked up because Wullie had to be escorted home drunk the evening before and put to bed. The front door opens and the local gossip and nosey neighbour Aggie Mooney enters.

'Yoo hoo, are youse decent?' she calls.

Shaking the newspaper with annoyance, Wullie mutters under his breath, 'It's that ould nuisance coming on her Sunday rounds to disturb the peace with her ould gossiping tongue.'

'Come on in, Aggie,' Cissy answered, throwing him a dirty look. 'I was just finishing the dishes and I'm going to put on the kettle for a cup of tae.'

'I see youse are all alone, how romantic,' chirps Aggie.

'Romantic my arse. Me up to my oxters in dishwater and him sitting there with a face that would cut coul iron. Sit down, Aggie, and tell us the bars, and don't be telling me anything sad, for God knows, I need a bit of cheering up the day.'

Wullie shakes his newspaper again to display his annoyance. 'Give me patience this day, O Lord,' he mumbles under his breath.

The two women ignore him. 'Wait till you hear these great bars, Cissy. You know yur man, Ricky Malley, from Bond Street?'

'Do you mean that clown "Tricky Ricky" who swims down at the quay now and then?' Cissy asks.

'Aye, that's him. Well, it seems he took up paintin.'

'What's so unusual about that, Aggie? Sure doesn't nearly everybody in Derry paint the front of their houses every June for St Columba's day?'

'Not that kind of paintin, Cissy. I mean real oil paintin, on a canvas and an easel with an artist's real paint brushes.'

'Are you serious, Aggie? I wouldn't have thought that Ricky Malley had any artistic tendencies. Sure the only art that he can do is sign his name with a pencil in the bru every Friday when he's lifting his dole.'

'It's the God's truth I'm telling you, Cissy, for I heard that he put an ad in last week's *Derry Journal* for a model to sit for him.'

'I read that ad myself, but it was in under the name of Richard and gave a box number. Are you sure it was Tricky Ricky?' asks Cissy.

'Aye it was Richard Malley all right, but wait till you hear the rest of it. It seems that yur woman Annie "Hacky Heels" from the lodgin house at the top of Bridge Street answered the advert and he told her that he was goin to paint her in the nude.'

'The dirty ould brute. Do you mean he was going to paint her without a stitch of clothing on him?'

'Naw, Cissy, *Ricky* wasn't going to be nude. He wanted Annie to pose in her birthday suit, and she agreed because he was payin her five shillins an hour.'

'She's not wise in the head anyway,' says Cissy. 'And did she take off all her clothes, then?' she asks, eager to hear more.

'Of course she did,' answers Aggie. 'Isn't that why I said that it was great bars?'

Lowering his newspaper, Wullie glowers over at Aggie. 'Here, that's enough of that ould chat in here, Aggie Mooney; you'd be better off saying yur prayers instead of scandalising people.'

'Just you houl yur tongue, Mr Goody-Goody Two-Shoes,' scowls Cissy. 'If *you* had been saying *yur* prayers yesterday evening instead of standing up the town half-cut and then ending up getting oxtered home by a policeman, you would be in a better mood the day.'

Wullie buries his face in his newspaper again without saying another word as she continues.

'Pay no heed to that ould crabbit shite, Aggie, go on and tell us the rest of the bars.'

'Where was I?' asks Aggie. 'Oh aye, it seems that Annie agreed to pose in the nude for Ricky and that he told her to go into the kitchen and get ready and he would put up his easel and mix up his paints. When he was ready he called Annie and she came out wearin only a pair of water boots.'

'My God, Aggie, that's hard to imagine,' gasps Cissy. 'Annie Hacky Heels standing naked and her wearing only a pair of water boots.'

'It's as true as I'm sittin here talkin to you, Cissy, and that's not the end of it, for when Ricky asked her why she decided to wear the water boots, she said that they would be handy for him to keep his paint brushes in.'

'That's a bit too hard to believe, Aggie. Whoever told you that ould yarn was only pullin yur leg.'

Aggie is feeling displeased with Cissy's attitude. 'Didn't we think that somebody was pullin our legs thon time we were told yur woman Sally McRafferty, from up around the Lone Moor Road, went to Dublin and posed in the nude for a boy to paint her and she was paid a wee fortune? Didn't everybody see her picture in one of the Sunday papers?'

'You're right enough, Aggie,' answers Cissy. 'And I'm sorry for disbelieving you. Do you think we'll see Annie Hacky Heels' picture in wan of the local papers some time?'

Aggie grins and glances towards Wullie. 'Maybe Wullie is sittin there now lookin at her picture in the *Sunday Journal*.'

Unable to hold his tongue any longer, Wullie angrily crumples up his newspaper and throws it on the floor. 'I'm not staying in here to listen to any more of yur ould bloody silly talk, Aggie Mooney,' he says in exasperation as he stomps out of the room slamming the door behind him.

'I've never seen Wullie in such a bad mood before,' says Aggie. 'What's the matter with him anyway?'

'He's still smarting since I give him a good bit of my tongue this morning. He'll get over it when he gets hungry again,' answers Cissy. 'Have you any more of them bars to tell me?'

Aggie answers with a giggle, 'I have, Cissy, but they will have to wait until later on this evenin after devotions.

When I'm on my way back from the chapel I'll drop in and tell them to you.'

With that, she leaves Cissy drying the dishes.

'Toodle-oo,' she says, closing the door softly behind her.

Bring Me the Sunset

Bring me the sunset in a cup of golden and fiery hue
And fetch me my pen that I may write of things
you never knew
Of how the lark's sweet song on high does make
our spirits soar
And of how the stars did show the way for
mariners of yore

I'll write of many creatures that dwell down in the deep
And why a weary soul seeks rest when all else are
fast asleep
Of how a seed that falls to earth will in time become a tree
And of even smaller living things that remain too small
to see

I'll tell of young hearts trembling beneath each
waxing moon
And of magic, coloured rainbows that dimmed,
alas, too soon
Of how a new-born infant's cries did make a house
a home
And of a partner's sharp-edged tongue that cut right
to the bone

Bring me the cup at eventide wherein the sunset rests
And I will write of gentle things that lie within
my breast
Of how two solid rings of gold once made two hearts
as one
And of how this one that's beating yet will fly before
the morn

Just a Country Boy

John, a modest and mannerly young man in his early twenties, lived with his widowed mother in a small cottage in the country near the Donegal border. An only child, he was not accustomed to travelling too far from his own locality, except when taking a weekly trip to Derry on a Wednesday, which was his day off from working in the small supermarket near his home.

John would have been easily recognised as a country boy by the way he went through the main streets, looking up in awe at the tall buildings and staring wide-eyed in the shop windows and at the traffic. Often, his mother would try to put him on his guard by cautioning him before he left home to catch the Derry bus.

'Watch out for those crafty Derry girls and boys who hang around the city centre, especially the ones from Creggan Estate and the Bogside, and don't let anybody see you looking at your money in the street, either, or they'll fleece you,' she would say.

John would smile in affection, knowing that his mother still looked on him as her baby boy. He would assure her by saying, 'Mother, don't be worrying yourself, I'm not a baby anymore, I'm twenty-two and quite able to outfox any of those Derry ones and, as a matter of fact, any other smart ass in our own locality as well.'

As usual one Wednesday, John took the bus and went on one of his rambles round Derry's city centre. He felt himself getting a little peckish and stopped to look in the window of a restaurant, where he enviously eyed the clients comfortably seated at their tables, eating delicious food and sipping wine. He then took an extreme fit of hunger as the overpowering, mouth-watering aromas of cooked food being expelled into the street through an extractor entered his sensitive nostrils, so much so that he felt he would faint if he went one step further.

John counted his money and, finding that he was carrying a little bit more than he usually did, made up his mind to go in and treat himself. *After all,* he thought, *it's about time I pampered myself for once instead of going into one of those wee pokey cafés to eat those greasy fries that I always get.*

Entering the restaurant, he looked around for a seat and spotted a waitress beckoning him to a table set for two. Once seated, he was given a menu, which he proceeded to browse through. *Not too bad these prices,* he thought. *I always imagined that the meals would be more expensive in one of these establishments.*

Just then, he heard a woman's voice directed at him.

'Excuse me, young man.'

He looked round, and an elderly lady seated on her own at the next table was looking at him with a friendly smile.

'Please excuse my intrusion, but you remind me of my son. He left home many years ago to settle in Australia and has never returned. You see, he died out there and I didn't even get to his funeral. His wife stopped writing to me long ago and I miss him terribly.'

'I'm sorry to hear that,' John sympathised and turned to his menu again.

The elderly lady spoke again.

'I wonder if you would do me a favour, son?'

John paused a moment before answering.

'If it's within my power and not too demanding, I might.'

The lady then asked if he would call her 'Mammy' and if she could join him at his table; that it would help to ease the longing she had for her son who so much resembled him.

John felt sorry for the elderly lady and invited her to sit with him, saying that he would be only too happy to call her Mammy, even if it would only give her a few minutes of happiness. And, as a matter of fact, she reminded him of his own mother at home.

She then insisted that she would pay for the meals and told John to order whatever he wanted, no matter how expensive it was. Eventually, the waitress came to their table.

'Now, Mammy,' said John, 'let's tell the nice waitress what you want to eat.'

They ordered their meals with wine and a bottle of the best vintage to take out as well. They both ate and drank and chatted, he calling her Mammy and she calling him wee son, until they had eaten and drunk to their hearts' content and John thinking all the while to himself, *Wait till I tell my mother about my luck and just how clever I have been getting this silly old lady to buy me an expensive meal and bottles of wine in a fancy restaurant. She'll be very proud and maybe a wee bit flabbergasted.*

The meal over, he excused himself, saying, 'I'm just going to the bathroom, Mammy, and I'll not be long.'

'That's fine, wee son,' the elderly lady said and, as he left the table, she called after him, 'and don't forget to wash your hands.'

John called back, 'I always do that anyway, Mammy.'

When John returned to the table from the toilet, the lady wasn't there but her bulging plastic shopping bag was on the chair.

'She must have gone to the toilet,' he said to himself and sat down.

Ten minutes later and there was no sign of the lady returning. John began to worry about her and asked a waitress to see if she was all right in the toilet.

The waitress looked at him in surprise and said, 'Your mammy left a little while ago and said that you would settle the bill.'

John nearly fell off the chair with shock and pointed to the shopping bag on the chair.

'I'm sure you must be mistaken, because there's her shopping still on the chair.'

At that, he reached over and lifted the bag and opened it. A look of immense shock and disbelief showed on his face when he saw what was in the shopping bag. John instantly realised that he had just been fleeced by a crafty and deceitful elderly woman, for inside the shopping bag was a whole load of old out-of-date newspapers and magazines. He sat gazing into the bag in amazement.

The waitress waited for him to say something when she realised that something was wrong.

'Are you feeling all right, there?'

John came back to reality.

'I'm feeling okay, thanks,' he answered in a slow, low voice, his eyes still staring into space as if he were in a trance.

'I'm sure your mother will explain her leaving before you returned to the table when you see her at home,' the waitress said, trying to comfort him.

'I have never seen that woman before in my life, and she isn't my mother. She asked me to call her Mammy just to make her feel happy because she said her son had passed away and that I resembled him and I, like a fool, felt sorry for her and now I'm left to pay for an expensive meal for two.' He looked into the bag again and let out a groan. 'The old vixen, she even had the nerve to take the bottle of expensive wine with her as well!'

What will my own mother think of me now? he thought. *After me saying that I was too smart for these Derry ones? I'll never live it down when everyone in my locality hears about it and makes a laughing stock of me.*

John explained his situation to the waitress, who brought the manager to his table. After a short discussion, the manager realised that John was a very decent but naive country boy and only charged him for the one meal, less the wine. It was a nice gesture on the manager's part and John left the restaurant, feeling quite satisfied. His reputation for being too smart for the Derry ones had been salvaged; now he could tell his mother and the locals that he had dined at a high-class establishment in Derry and got two expensive meals with wine at a greatly reduced price.

Standing at the bus stop later that evening, John watched the people passing to and fro on their various missions. He happened to notice a Mercedes Benz car parked opposite and an elderly lady opening the door. She got into the driver's seat, put the seat belt on and started the engine. She pulled the car out slowly from the kerb and, as she did so, spotted John watching her. John's mouth dropped open in disbelief as the old lady kissed the palm of her hand and blew the kiss towards him. She then mouthed a few words towards him: 'Bye-bye, wee son,' before she drove off, smiling serenely.

John's hand involuntarily rose and waved back as he mouthed in return, 'Bye-bye, Mammy.' He had to pinch himself in case he had just been daydreaming.

John boarded his bus for home and flopped limply down on an empty seat, where he breathed a long sigh of tiredness. *I'll not be too hasty in turning a deaf ear to my mother's wise words in future,* he thought, *because I'm still just a country boy at heart and I have just learned a costly lesson today in the University of Life.*

The Lost Boys

The city-centre café was getting busy with its usual stream of patrons who began to occupy its tables for their usual afternoon snacks. It followed the same pattern every day: lady pensioners meeting to pass an hour and chat; a handful of diners who liked to sit quietly on their own, reading their newspapers or just looking out the window at the passing pedestrians and traffic; or maybe couples, some of whom talked low to one another or just ate in silence.

Tony Newman, a fifty-something, tidily dressed, potbellied, balding Englishman, locally seen as a loner, sat sipping tea from his near-empty cup. His meal was finished and his mobile phone lay on the table. The phone rang and he immediately picked it up. 'Hello, Tony here.' He paused for a second or two. 'Irene? Yes, Irene, I'm here in the café. See you in a while, then.'

He rose and went to the Gents to tidy his hair and wash his hands. Some minutes later, he returned to his table. He spotted her coming through the entrance and signalled. The description she had given him a few days earlier over the phone was accurate. Irene Stephens, a tall, slim and pretty looking middle-aged lady with flecks of grey in her short, dark hair, approached him. It was through a looking-for-a-lost-relative letter in a local newspaper that Irene and Tony first met.

Irene was married with two teenage children and lived in Belfast. Her parents had passed away three years before and she was searching for information about her only brother, Barney Melly, who had left home twenty years ago when he was sixteen. He had written home a few years later informing his parents that he was in London and was getting married to a nice girl with wealthy parents. He was working in a hotel and would bring his wife over to Belfast sometime to meet the rest of his family. The years had gone by and not a word had been heard from him since. Exhaustive attempts were made on the family's behalf by various people to contact him in London over the intervening years, but to no avail.

However, Irene had recently received some important information about her brother from a work colleague who came from Derry and who travelled home every weekend. He told her that one Saturday evening he had fallen into conversation with a man in a bar in Derry who told him that he had once lived in Belfast. The man calling himself Barney Melly told him that he had run away from home when he was sixteen and had never returned there since. Barney said that he drifted around England for years and was about to come home again to Belfast but came to Derry instead when he learned that his parents had passed away. He hadn't the heart to face his only sister, Irene, whose married name was Stephens and who he believed still lived somewhere in Belfast. That was what prompted Irene to write to a Derry newspaper to inquire about her brother and Tony Newman had contacted her.

They shook hands and he introduced himself. 'I'm

Tony Newman, won't you have a chair?' She sat down and he ordered two cups of tea. 'You said that your brother in his last letter home to your parents said that he was married?'

Irene replied, 'Yes, but he told my work friend that he only made that up to keep our parents from worrying about him.'

Tony said that he understood why her brother had told her parents that he was getting on fine in London. 'I went through the same experience myself after I ran away from my home in England to live here in Ireland and drifted around from town to town. I, too, pretended that I was in a good job and wrote home after ten years to say I was married, just to make my parents happy and to keep them from searching for me. I am still a loner, never trusting anyone and afraid to make friends with people in case they discover the lies I had told to my family. I believe that both my parents are passed on by now.'

They talked for a little longer until Irene asked Tony if he believed that her brother was now living in Derry. Tony told her that he had spoken lately to a person with a slight Belfast accent called Barney Melly, who told him that he had been drifting around England for years and was now living rough in Derry and staying in and old abandoned house on the outskirts of the town along with a couple of other men.

Irene was elated on hearing this piece of news. 'It must be Barney, I'm sure of it,' she said excitedly. 'Do you know where the house is or where I could find him today?'

Tony hesitated before answering her questions. 'I know the house, but I don't think it would be right to take you there. I think it would be wiser if I were to look for him first around the town and go to the usual places where other men like Barney are known to frequent.'

Irene agreed and they arranged to meet again in another hour at the café. Until then, she would browse the shops to pass the time.

***

Tony returned to the café just over an hour later and told Irene that her brother hadn't been seen around all morning.

'What about the house that he stays in? Could you give me directions so that I might go and see if he's there?' she asked.

Tony replied, 'Look, let's have a cup of tea and wait for a while just in case we see him passing.'

Irene could do nothing else but take his advice.

Another hour had passed and still no sign of the Belfast man; Irene began to get unsettled. 'I've waited here long enough,' she said impatiently. 'Would you please tell me how to get to that house so that I can be on my way? You must understand that I have to drive back home again to my family in Belfast this evening.'

Tony offered to go along with Irene in her car and she warily agreed, thinking that she would just have to trust this man, this loner whom she'd only just met. In the car, he gave her directions until they were on a straight country road. Irene kept silent all the way, feeling her heart beating a little faster than it usually did through anticipation and fear of what danger could lie in store for her. Her mind was turning things over and she was thinking, *What if this man is lying to me? What if he and the so-called Belfast man have planned to get me alone in an empty house far out in the country? Should I stop the car at the next house I see and ask for help, or am I just being paranoid?*

Irene was still feeling nervous as they neared a house up ahead and she resolved to pull up beside it and go and knock on the front door for safety's sake.

Just as Irene slowed down and began to pull in to the side of the road in front of the house, Tony spoke. 'That's the house now; you can pull into the driveway and wait for me there while I go inside.' Irene didn't pull into the driveway but instead parked on the road so that any passing motorist would see the car. *Better to be seen in case something goes wrong,* she thought. Tony got out of the car without commenting on her reason for not going into the driveway. 'I shouldn't be too long,' was all he said.

He remained inside for what seemed to Irene an eternity. She tooted the horn and a strange face appeared at the window of the house. A few more moments had passed and Tony emerged. He approached the car, opened the door and gestured for Irene to follow him.

Irene resisted for a moment before asking, 'Am I in any danger? Please tell me.'

On realising that she was afraid, Tony smiled broadly. 'Of course you are in no danger, Irene. I'm sorry if I made you feel that you were. Please accept my apologies.'

Irene felt more relaxed on hearing Tony's friendly reassurance and got out of the car. They went towards the house and Tony went in first to make her feel more at ease. Still feeling slightly apprehensive, she followed him into a damp-smelling room at the back of the house where a shabbily dressed middle-aged man was seated on a worn-out settee. The man, looking nervous, stood up and Tony introduced him to Irene.

'This is Barney Melly,' he said. And to the man, he said, 'Meet Irene Stephens, who I believe from what you have just been telling me is your sister.'

Irene and Barney stood silently, looking at each other for a number of seconds.

Tony moved his gaze from one to the other until Irene broke the tension with a cry of joy on recognising her brother. She rushed forward and put her arms around Barney, who did likewise. A lost brother and sister had found each other after all those years, thanks to a loner called Tony Newman.

Tony Newman stood motionless and exhaled a sigh of relief; a small teardrop trickled down his cheek. He had helped a complete stranger find her long-lost brother and prayed that someday, somehow, someone belonging to himself would find him.

Revenge at the Funeral Home

Did you ever wonder what it would be like to be kept inside a funeral parlour all night? I suppose you would be forgiven for asking how people could manage to get themselves into such a predicament unless they worked there and somehow were accidentally locked in at closing time by some other work colleague. Well, I can tell you that it happens every day of the week, all over the world, because, you see, those poor unfortunates happen to have passed away and lie waiting there in fancily decorated wooden boxes to be dispatched on their final farewells from this world by their loved ones.

Herbie Hogan, at twenty-one years of age, had begun his fifth month as a taxi driver for Jack McGarvey's Undertakers. His previous jobs since leaving school included delivering groceries, car washing, bar tending, window cleaning and serving meals in a McDonald's fast-food establishment. Having gone through all of those learning experiences, it was no wonder that Herbie exuded an extremely outgoing happy-go-lucky personality that soon made him many friends among the other taxi drivers and clients.

Herbie, on occasion when the mood took him, was known to display somewhat giddy actions of self-expression. One such mood came over him one day when he was sitting in his taxi at a standstill in a traffic jam. He got so amused at some of the other bad-tempered drivers blowing their horns that he climbed onto the roof of his taxi and sang a medley of happy songs that included *When You're Smiling* at the top of his voice. When he finished singing, all the other drivers tooted their horns to show their appreciation to him for entertaining them. Often on paydays, he would dance his boss Jack around the office to express his feelings of gratitude for employing him. The boss, red-faced with embarrassment in front of the other employees, would threaten to get rid of him. Of course, Jack McGarvey was really trying to keep from laughing out loud.

That was Herbie Hogan, so extrovert and self-expressive to the extreme that he should have been an actor.

One day, Herbie and two of his co-workers were exchanging tales about some of the more amusing experiences they had encountered while attending funerals. Stories such as the male passenger who insisted on the cab waiting outside a local pub while he and his fellow mourners went in to have a last drink to their dead colleague who was on his final trip to the cemetery. And the little old lady who wanted her husband buried face down so that he wouldn't be able to look at the nice scenery to be seen from the City Cemetery where he would be buried. Or the unforgiving husband who requested the vicar call for 'three cheers' and 'hip, hip, hooray' at the graveside of his unfaithful spouse. And then there was the one about the drunk who was taking a shortcut through the graveyard on his way home from the pub one night and fell into a freshly dug grave, where he fell asleep. A few hours later, another drunken man was taking a shortcut through the same graveyard when he heard a man chattering through his teeth saying that he was cold. The second man looked into the grave and, on seeing the other drunk lying shivering, said, 'It's no wonder you're freezing – sure you've kicked all the clay off yourself.' That story got Herbie to thinking of a good practical joke to play on his workmates. He thought it might be a good idea to lie inside a coffin and pull the lid over it and wait for one of his colleagues to lift it off and get the shock of his life when Herbie would shout 'Boo!' and reach for him.

It so happened that one evening Herbie was asked to work late in the funeral-parlour workshop to help the resident carpenter to prepare some coffins for use the next morning. The carpenter, Ted Dunn, was a deaf mute and had never quite taken to Herbie. He didn't understand Herbie's playful antics and mistakenly believed that sometimes Herbie was trying to make a fool of him.

They worked together that evening in silence, inserting the coffin linings and fixing the handles on and screwing the nameplates on the lids until it was time to go home. It was then that Ted went to the bathroom to wash up and Herbie decided to try out one of the coffins for size and climbed in. Herbie didn't know that Ted was watching him through the slightly open door, and when he believed Herbie was lying comfortably inside the coffin, he slipped out of the front door of the funeral parlour and locked it. Ted was pleased with himself that he had placed Herbie in a predicament. He would wait outside for ten minutes, holding the door handle and wait to feel Herbie trying to open it in a panic. He would hold his hand against the door and feel it being battered and kicked and enjoy the fear he knew would be gripping Herbie.

Ted waited a quarter of an hour, but no vibrations or handle-rattling materialised. He was now wondering what had happened to Herbie and quietly went back into the parlour. There he got the surprise of his life when he found Herbie fast asleep in the coffin. Now was Ted's really big chance to repay Herbie for all the presumed insults and mockeries that he suffered since coming to work there. Ted went about his task quietly, placing the lid on the coffin and turning down the four brass wing nuts, but not overly tight, for he wouldn't want him to suffocate altogether through lack of air. Herbie, unaware of his fate, was lying contentedly slumbering inside. Ted couldn't wait to let his colleagues know that he had locked him in all night and see Herbie's face in the morning when they opened the coffin.

Next morning, Herbie was woken from a deep slumber by the noise of a heavy door-lock being activated and the squeaking of hinges. He found himself in complete darkness, forgetting where he was. *Holy Mother of God,* he thought, *I must have been asleep for a long time.* He rubbed his eyes and suddenly became aware that he was lying on his back in a very confined space. *What the hell?* he muttered as he tried to sit upright, bumping his face against the coffin lid. He touched it with his hand and felt the grain of the wood. *Where in heaven's name am I?* he thought, scratching about for a handle or an opening. Then he remembered and started to scream in terror. 'Help, help! Somebody let me out of here. I'm here in this coffin and somebody has screwed down the lid.' Not having enough room to hammer with his fists, Herbie tapped the lid with his knuckles, hoping that somebody would hear him and release him from his wooden prison before he suffocated. 'Help, help! Get me out of here!' Herbie yelled at the top of his voice, only to be answered by his own muffled shouts reverberating back at him. *Nobody can hear me through the thick wooden box,* he thought. *Is there no-one in the funeral parlour to save me?* Herbie then realised that the coffin was being lifted and he could feel it moving along on castors until it came to rest again. Soon the swaying motions and the vibrations thrumming through the bottom of the coffin told him he was being driven somewhere. *I must be in a hearse on the way to the graveyard,* he thought in horror.

Herbie knew, too, when the hearse had stopped and he sensed the coffin being taken out and carried to the graveside. He could hear the prayers being offered up for the repose of a soul and he could hear the ropes being inserted through the coffin's handles in preparation to be lowered into the freshly dug grave. He lay surprisingly calm and resigned to his fate when he heard the spade full of clay drumming on the lid and a faint muffled voice praying, 'Thou art dust and unto dust thou shall return.' It was then that he realised that he was about to be buried alive and began to scream in terror again and kick at the bottom panel of the coffin. He continued kicking until he put his feet through it and a beam of light rushed in to blind him for a second or two. It was then he heard the laughter from his colleagues and the lid being unscrewed and removed. Herbie sat up to find that he was in the small back garden of the funeral home and his workmates, including his boss, were gathered round him, all of them laughing.

He climbed out, cursing and swearing. 'What are you fecking bunch of lunatics up to, nearly scaring me to death?'

When they had had their fill of laughing, Jack McGarvey told him how they had faked his burial. 'When we arrived this morning, Ted let us know that you had fallen sound asleep inside one of the coffins last night and that he had put on the lid for a joke. I knew you were woken by the noise of the door-bolt being pulled open, for I could hear you tapping on the inside of the coffin lid. Then we carried the coffin out to the hearse and drove it around to the garden here to fake your funeral.'

Everyone started laughing again and Herbie responded, 'You mad eejits. And as for you, Ted Dunn, I didn't even think you were capable of pulling a prank like that.'

Ted stood looking at Herbie with a blank expression on his face and with his mouth hanging open. He gradually got the gist of what was said to him and mimicked a hearty laugh by smiling broadly while holding his arms around his stomach. Ted had got his revenge on Herbie … and he was enjoying it.

Herbie couldn't help but laugh out loud at Ted's funny gesture and they became firm friends at McGarvey's Undertakers from that day on.

Delight, Sorrow and Pain

A child has arrived, a brother for you all, with tiny
hands and feet
And nose so small and eyes of distant blue and wispy
hair of gold
Can I touch him, can I hold him, will he break if I do,
and will he cry?
Did straight he come from heaven, our little angel,
will we thank God, too?
I remember our joy and glee that beautiful day,
that lovely day he was born
With chrism of oil and holy water our spoonful
of delight was blessed
Those two short happy years have passed since
I learned that he was not like me
Nor would ever be, for a Down's syndrome special
baby was he
For God to take back at will and plunge our hearts
into a course of sorrow

In this sunlit place by my window I sit, wrapped
in a gown of quiet contented peace
Only the ticking of the clock on the mantelpiece
shelf to regulate

And record the life that is, and passing on
Mother softly singing while she tidies the room
to a new day
In the other room, a bedroom where a baby
boy-child sleeps
The curtains silently close to end his part,
an angel in life's drama
No drums, no trumpets to sound a farewell
Only the ticking of a mantelpiece clock heralds the
passing and re-birth of an angel

This knot of pain that has gripped my heart for
this burden of grief that I bear
That will not loosen, that will not give me ease
from this unending sorrow
This unbearable gnawing anguish in my soul and mind,
this choking swell in my throat
And yet still no tears have I shed to console my breast,
no teardrops to fall
No crying
No relief to soothe this longing ache to let
my heart rest

A Holy Ghost

Paul was a lively 19-year-old Magee College student, born and raised in Derry. He had befriended Dan, who came from the village of Greencastle in County Donegal and who was also a student at Magee. They had been planning and preparing for a summer cycling holiday around Ireland since Christmas, cycling nearly forty miles every weekend – weather permitting – to reach the fitness levels needed for the long journey. It was now midsummer and Paul and Dan were halfway through their cycling tour.

Having left the town of Castlebar early in the morning, they travelled through the craggy Mayo countryside, near the west coast of Ireland, and by late evening were about seven miles from the small hamlet of Pontoon, which nestled between Lough Con and Lough Cullin. Heavy, grey rain clouds burdened the sky, bringing on an early darkness over the heather-covered landscape. As they sped down a steep hill towards Pontoon and a welcome shelter for the night in a backpackers' hostel, large drops of rain began stinging their faces. They stopped and donned their wet gear and continued for another few miles. However, luck wasn't with them, as Dan's front tyre suddenly deflated and he steered his cycle to the side of the road and the shelter of a high hawthorn hedge. Paul, realising what had happened, went back to assist him. The rain was now bouncing off the road as they examined the punctured tyre and found that it was torn and needed replaced.

'Head you on into Pontoon,' Dan said to Paul. 'I'll walk the rest of the way and meet you at the hostel. Sure it can't be much more than three miles away.'

Paul, assured in the knowledge that his friend would be safe and well, carried on, leaving Dan walking steadily downhill, pushing his cycle.

It was raining steady and Dan could hear distant rumbles of thunder echoing through the hills. *What a miserable evening to be walking through this strange, empty wilderness,* he thought as a flash of lightning reflected off the distant Lough Con. It was getting darker now and he could see the twinkling lights of a small village or hamlet about three or four miles distant that might well be Pontoon. He couldn't wait to shed his wet gear and get a warm shower and something to eat before retiring early to a nice comfortable hostel bed.

The rain began to fall more gently as he plodded on, and the rumbles of thunder he could still hear now seemed to be coming from a greater distance, which made him feel more at ease. *Thank goodness that thunderstorm is moving away from here,* he thought, feeling his spirits lighten in tune with the rain. As he walked on, his ears picked up the droning sound of a car engine coming from some distance behind him. The sound gradually grew louder and he moved to the verge of the road just as the headlights of a car brightened up the roadway ahead. It stopped beside him and the male driver rolled down his window and spoke.

'Having problems cycling?' the driver asked.

'I have a puncture in the front tyre and it needs replaced,' answered Dan.

'Have you got far to go?'

'About three or four more miles or so.'

'I could give you a lift part of the way if you like, and I have a double cycle rack on the back of the car,' the driver informed him. 'There's another bicycle on the rack, belonging to another young man whom I gave a lift to recently, but he went off somewhere and never returned to collect it.'

Dan accepted the offer and the driver secured the cycle on the rack. Once inside the car again, he introduced himself. 'I'm Pastor Jones, a preacher of the good news, and I'm just touring about this part of the country, bringing the word of the four gospels to these poor pagan people. I'm on my way to the village of Foxford, but I am going to stop at the next village for the night should you wish to join me.'

Dan thanked the preacher and told him that his friend would be waiting for him at a hamlet called Pontoon. The preacher said that he didn't know where Pontoon was and that Dan would have to get off at the next stop, the village of Drumbane, where he might get his tyre replaced.

They continued in silence until Dan saw the signpost Drumbane on his side of the road and shortly thereafter they arrived at the village which, strangely, showed no sign of light in any window. Indeed, it would have been virtually pitch-dark except for the lights from the car. 'This is Drumbane, where we both get out,' said the preacher.

Dan's heart leapt to his throat. 'But where can I get

my cycle repaired in this abandoned-looking place?' he asked. 'There's only one street and that looks as if it's completely deserted.'

The preacher didn't answer immediately but turned off the car lights and stepped out of the car. The moon showed through a break in the clouds and the misting rain gave the street a fleetingly eerie look. 'You're quite correct,' answered the preacher finally. 'This is an abandoned village and I'm afraid you will have to stay here until it gets light again at dawn.'

He began taking Dan's bicycle from the rack and as he did so he started singing a well-known hymn called *The Old Rugged Cross*. Standing the bicycle against a wall, while leaving the other one on the rack, he called out, 'There you are, son,' and continued singing. 'I will cling to the old rugged cross, and exchange it some day for a crown.'

Dan shivered, not knowing what to do, and said thanks. Should he take the preacher's advice and stay in this eerie-looking place until the morning or leave his bike here and start walking again in the hope of getting another lift? *Paul will be worrying about me and might come back along the road in search of me,* he thought, *and he, too, might get into difficulties on his own.* He felt uneasy, but because of the uncertain weather and darkness and the thought of carrying his heavy rucksack – which contained all his personal belongings and dry clothes – he decided to stay with the preacher, who was now opening the door of a vacant house. The preacher had a bright torch and searched around inside for a lamp or other source of light. On finding an oil lamp on a shelf just inside the door, he lit the wick, and a small, sparsely furnished, musty-smelling room sprung to life.

'Here we are,' he said. 'Isn't this better than walking those dark, wet roads at this time of night?'

'It looks comfortable enough,' answered Dan, 'but who owns the house?'

'Nobody,' answered the preacher. 'I've been here many times before and have never met a single sinner. Make yourself comfortable and I'll fix us a snack.'

He went into a small scullery, where he lit another lamp. 'I'm looking for a spare cup and plate for you,' he called back to Dan, who was now sitting on a tattered, battered old sofa. As the preacher busied himself taking some foodstuffs from his bag, he began to quote from the scriptures: 'And Moses led his people into the desert and each morning they fed on manna that fell to earth from heaven during the night. Repent all you sinners for the end is nigh. Glory, glory, hallelujah!' He yelled the last line!

Startled, Dan sat and listened as the pastor then started preaching about the miracle of the loaves and fishes and about Jesus spending forty days in the wilderness, living on locusts and wild honey. Further loud bible quotes followed: 'Leave all your worldly possessions and your families, take up your cross and follow me and you will enter the Kingdom of Heaven.'

On and on his voice droned until it began to reverberate inside Dan's head. He could take no more of it. Here he was, stranded in a strange house in an empty village that was miles from civilisation with this raving religious head-case while his friend, Paul, would be waiting and worrying about him in a nice, comfortable hostel in Pontoon. He pressed his cupped hands against his ears in an attempt to block out the preacher's manic utterances, but to no avail.

Dan was at the end of his tether and shouted, 'Agggggh! Would you for Jesus' sake shut your mouth for a while, you crazy raving lunatic, before you drive me as mad as yourself with your bloody preaching and singing. Shut up, shut up, shut up, you madman.'

The preacher was stunned into silence on hearing Dan and slowly came in from the scullery with a large bread knife in one hand and a bread roll in the other. He pointed the gleaming knife threateningly at Dan and began to quote yet another piece of scripture while waving the bread roll in the air: 'Those who spurn the words of the Evangelist will perish in the everlasting flames of Hell. Open your ears and listen and you will be saved.' He started to sing again at the top of his voice: 'Onward, Christian soldiers, marching as to war, with the cross of Jesus going on before.'

Dan sat motionless, about to make a dash for the door if the preacher came any nearer, but the cleric wheeled around and went back to the scullery again, leaving Dan wondering what he should do. Then he remembered about the map inside the pack tied to his cycle and he quietly and swiftly went outside to fetch it.

The rain had stopped and the moon now lit up the scene, a long muddy roadway flanked by grey, drab, uninteresting buildings that looked as if they had been vacated many years ago. No light showed from any doorway or window. *A ghost town indeed,* he thought as a shiver went up and down his spine. He went back into the house, with the map. The preacher was still singing loudly in the scullery.

Dan sat down and opened the map; a sheet of paper fell from between its folds. Then he remembered that it was a memo of the route that Paul had written for him before leaving on their tour. He read down the list of all the places of interest they had passed or stopped in since leaving Derry. It named everywhere they had been, including their last overnight stop, Castlebar, before setting out to continue their journey that morning to Pontoon, which was to be their next planned stop for the night. There was no other hamlet or village showing on the list or on the map. However, a footnote at the bottom of the memo read: 'A mock village called Drumbane had been built just two miles from Pontoon by an American film company forty years ago and only one building was completed for the indoor scenes, the others being empty facades. Drumbane was demolished one year after the filming was finished.'

This, then, must be the only habitable building, and it's only two miles from Pontoon, thought Dan. He was puzzled. *But Paul also said that it had been demolished years ago.* Just then, the preacher entered from the scullery, carrying two mugs of tea and a plateful of buttered bread. He was singing another hymn now: 'The Lord is my shepherd, I shall not want.'

Dan thought to himself, *There's a big bloody want in you, you crazy head bin.*

The preacher said Grace and they ate their meal in silence. He then took a small bible from his pocket and began to read from the Old Testament according to John. After listening for a few minutes, Dan dropped off to sleep with the preacher's monotonous voice fading in his ears.

He woke to find the preacher gone from the room. It was now 4.30 AM and all was silent. He tiptoed to the bedroom and peeped in. The preacher was fast asleep in one of two single beds, the silence broken only by his light breathing. *This is my chance to leave this godforsaken place now that I know where I am,* thought Dan, and he quietly slipped out the front door into the night. The pale moon's light was now waning as a narrow ribbon of a silver dawn silhouetted the tops of the hills. Dan removed the other bicycle from the cycle rack. It was much older than his bike but, the tyres seemed okay and, after inserting a new tube that he had carried as part of his repairs equipment, he exchanged his damaged tyre for the better one. He hastily scribbled a note and tucked it under the windscreen wiper. It read: 'Thanks for the lift and for the tea, Pastor Jones.'

I took the front tyre off the other bike with God's aid and with an old religious phrase in mind that I'm sure you yourself have said many times: 'The Lord helps those who help themselves.'

Not a sound came from the house as Dan mounted and rode away from the village. He was about two hundred yards away and stopped at a crossroads where the signpost pointed to Pontoon. The brightening dawn was slowly creeping across the sky and dun-coloured landscape as he checked back along the road in case the preacher had awakened and decided to follow him. He nearly fell off his saddle and shivered as the hairs stood on the back of his neck: where the 'mock village' of Drumbane had been only a few minutes before he now saw only the rusted pieces of what were once a car and a bicycle protruding from barren bogland.

It was a ghost town all right, just as I thought when I arrived here with that peculiar preacher last night, Dan said to himself matter-of-factly before cycling away from the crossroads to continue and complete his journey to Pontoon and his friend Paul.

Truancy and Trouting

Don and Eddie were schoolboy chums who had planned to play truant and go trout fishing at the lake on the island two miles away from their village of Burnfoot. It was a fresh, sunny May morning and each carried bread and bottles of water in their school satchels. They had hidden their school books in Jimmy Mitchell's cowshed and would collect them on their way home again in the evening.

'It's a good morning for fishing, Eddie. Have you got the tin of worms?' Don asked.

'I have and all, Don. I turned over a pile of old rotten dung at the end of the byre yesterday evening and must have gotten nearly a hundred of them. If we get a trout for every worm, we'll make a fortune selling them on Friday.'

A light breeze rippled the surface of the water as they cycled round the lake to hide their bicycles in a little copse of willows; it would also provide cover for them in case old Sam Wray passed along the road. He lived alone in a shabby-looking cottage with a rusted, corrugated-tin roof at the head of the lane above the road.

On arriving at the edge of the lake and full of excitement, they assembled their fishing rods and baited their hooks with the wriggling red dung worms. 'Here goes,' said Don, casting his line into the lake.

'Here goes me, too,' said Eddie as he executed a cast that landed with a splash not too far from Don's. They rested the tips of their rods on a couple of large stones and sat down on a flat rock to watch and wait for the tell-tale signs of trout nibbling at the worms.

For fifteen minutes they watched and waited, with no results, until Don stood up and said, 'It's probably too bright yet for the fish to bite.'

Eddie agreed, saying, 'I often heard my da say the same thing when he took me fishing.'

They waited restlessly for another ten minutes before deciding to walk a hundred yards round the shore to examine a small rowing boat that lay on its side in the reeds. On their way along the water's edge, they examined various pieces of flotsam that lay along there – pieces of wood, bottle corks, a shoe and a sheep's horn lay scattered among the stones – but a sealed glass bottle with something inside was the only item that really aroused their curiosity. Don opened it and shook out a crumpled piece of paper. He smoothed it out and saw some writing, which he read aloud: 'Anyone who reads this note has just invited bad luck on themselves.' It was signed: Esmeralda, the Witch of the Island. 'Some silly person must have written this,' he said with a laugh.

Eddie wasn't smiling. 'I wouldn't take it too lightly, Don. You never know, there might just be such a witch as Esmeralda. I think you should push the note back into the bottle, fill it with water and throw it back into the lake again to break the bad-luck spell.'

Don stopped smiling. 'Maybe you're right, Eddie. Just to be on the safe side.' He did as Eddie suggested, saying,

'Good riddance to you and your bad luck, Esmeralda.'

They then continued along the shore, examining other bits and pieces until, as they neared the boat, Don picked up a broken length of a varnished, blackthorn stick.

'This might just be a piece of one of Esmeralda's old broomsticks,' he said jokingly and they both laughed.

'It would be a bit painful for her to sit on if it were a broom handle,' said Eddie, making them laugh more.

When they reached the boat, the friends casually looked into it and immediately ran back in fright to where their rods were. Don, still gripping the piece of blackthorn stick, was first to speak in short, breathless syllables.

'Jeepers creepers! Did you see his face?'

Eddie, nearly in tears, answered, 'Aye, I think it was ould Sam Wray and his head was bleeding. Do you think he's dead?'

'I don't think so, Eddie. I'm sure he opened his eyes and looked at me; that's what scared me most.'

'That message in the bottle was for real, all right, and this must be the bad-luck spell beginning to take effect. What are we going to do?' Eddie asked. 'Should we get our rods and bikes and head back to the crossroads?'

Don answered him in a worried tone. 'It might be better to go over to the boat again to have another look. If ould Sam is ill or injured, he'll need help. And if we abandon him, he might die.'

They decided to return to the boat and, fetching their satchels, went back again hesitantly to see if there was anything they could do. Warily, they approached the boat and peered in. It was old Sam, right enough, lying on his back with his legs dangling over the seat. He was bleeding from a head wound and groaned on seeing the two bewildered boys staring wide-eyed down at him. 'Help me,' he muttered painfully in a weak rasping voice.

Don and Eddie were ready to run away again with fear but they stood as if frozen to the spot.

'Help me up, lads, I think my back must be broken,' pleaded poor old Sam in a stronger voice this time.

Don quickly took a bottle of water from his satchel. He reached into the boat, put his hand under Sam's head and gave him a sip of water.

Eddie stepped into the boat and caught Sam by the hands. 'We'll pull you up onto the seat if you can help us,' he said. 'Do you think you could do that?'

Old Sam lifted his head and pulled hard on Eddie's hands as Don pushed from behind and, with a great deal of huffing and puffing, they managed to get him sitting upright. He stretched his back a few times and slowly moved his shoulders forwards and backwards.

'Thanks, boys. I thought my back was broken when I became conscious again and didn't want to move until I regained my full mental faculties. Now help me out of the boat and walk with me to me cottage.' With the boys' help, he managed to stand and climb out of the boat. 'My cottage is at the top of that there laneway,' he said, nodding his head in the direction of the cottage with the rusted corrugated tin roof.

They walked him slowly up the lane and he told them how he had come to be lying in the boat. 'Early this morning, I was ready to go fishing on the lake and was about to push the boat out of the shallows when someone came behind me from out of the tall reeds and struck me on the head with a stick or something.' He winced as he touched the back of his head and continued. 'As I fell, I saw someone dressed in black retreating into the reeds again. Then I lost consciousness and lay there until I heard you two boys talking and splashing about in the shallow water.'

Don and Eddie told Sam about finding the bottle with Esmeralda's bad-luck note about the spell inside it. Old Sam managed a faint smile. 'Pay no heed to it, that's them ould silly notes that that ould Biddy Cairns leaves all over the place. She lives alone in an ould abandoned caravan in the corner of a field not too far from here. She's quite mad and thinks she's a witch.' He scratched the stubble on his chin with his fingertips. 'Now that I think about it, I'm sure it was Biddy who struck me on the head, the crazy ould crone.' The two boys listened, eyes wide with excitement and a hint of fear on their faces as Sam continued speaking. 'She's been telling people that I'm living here in her cottage, that it once belonged to her father and that I put her out after he died forty years ago. Of course, it's untrue, because I was reared there along with my two brothers and a sister, all of whom moved away from the island many years ago.'

He went quiet again and then Don remembered the piece of blackthorn stick that he had picked up along the shore and carried with him. He showed it to Sam. 'Do you think this is what ould Biddy hit you with, Sam? It was lying not far from the boat.'

Sam gently put his fingers to his wound, which had now stopped bleeding. 'Well, if that's not a good wan,' he exclaimed, taking the piece of blackthorn stick in his hand to examine it. 'I'll be damned,' he said, surprised. 'This is newly broken and is heavy enough to break an elephant's skull.' He paused for a moment in thought before speaking again. 'Ould Biddy must have broken her blackthorn stick when she struck me on the head and cleared off with the other piece in her hand.'

Don and Eddie kept silent. They were feeling uncomfortable and scared now, knowing that they were already in trouble for playing truant from school. Even worse, they didn't even have one trout to show for all their troubles.

Now nearing the top of the lane, Sam was feeling faint again. The boys helped him to stand upright and Don gave him another sip of water. They helped him along until they reached the cottage entrance. Sam suddenly stopped and stared at it. The door was wide open.

'What in heaven's name?' he exclaimed, moving himself forward from the boys. He shakily entered the cottage and slowed just inside the door, Don and Eddie cautiously following him. The sun was shining in through a small window, brightening up most of the interior except for one corner that remained in shadow beside the open hearth, where a fire of turf smouldered. In the unlit corner, a dark form sat on Sam's wooden armchair, causing the three of them to gasp and stand still on seeing it.

Sam, recognising who it was, spoke first. 'It's you, Biddy Cairns, you ould hag. What the blazes do you think you are up to, breaking into my home, you ould witch?' He paused, waiting for a reply, but there was no response. 'It was you who tried to kill me down at the lake this morning.' Yet no voice answered and none of the four, including Biddy, moved, although Don and Eddie were ready to bolt out of the place.

The pale face of Biddy Cairns became more visible now that their eyes had become accustomed to looking into the dark corner. Biddy just sat still as a statue, eerily staring at them, her eyes reflecting the red, smouldering embers of the fire, which made her indeed look like some devilish being.

Sam watched the red glow pulsing in her eyes and felt uneasy by her silence. He could hear his heart pounding loudly in his ears and began to approach her slowly while raising the piece of heavy blackthorn stick to his shoulder height.

'I'm still alive and kicking, Biddy,' he hissed through his clenched, rotting teeth. Biddy stayed there motionless, brazen as brass, her red eyes still staring. The bile and fear got up in old Sam and he swiftly struck Biddy on the shoulder with the stick, shouting, 'Get out of my house, you crazy ould divil of a witch. Get out before I knock your brains out.'

Don and Eddie dashed out into the yard, where they stood peeping in through the small window at the two old enemies, Sam and Biddy, confronting each other, she unmoving in the chair and he with the stick now raised above his head in readiness to strike again if she should make one move.

Slowly, Biddy Cairns's eerie-looking dark form began to move slowly forward in the chair. Sam was startled and stepped back a pace. As he did, he brought the stick down hard, missing Biddy's head by an inch as she fell with a dull thud onto the dusty flagstone floor.

As Don and Eddie witnessed this, they took to their heels and were halfway down the lane when they heard Sam calling on them to come back. They stopped running. 'Now we're in real trouble,' winced Eddie as they reluctantly returned to the cottage.

Sam told them that Biddy Cairns had been sitting dead in the chair all the time. 'She must be dead a couple of hours,' he said, 'because she's as stiff as a piece of salted dried ling fish that you would see hanging up in McIvor's grocery shop.' He said it without any feelings of sympathy for the poor old, mentally disturbed woman who now lay dead, a misshapen cold figure on the hard, stone floor.

Don and Eddie were both shaking nervously when Sam told them to cycle to the village and notify the Guards and the local priest. Obediently, the two bewildered boys set off to face their fate. For heaven only knew what lay in store for the two young lads who had innocently stayed away from school one fresh sunny May morning to catch trout in the island lake and found themselves caught up in a real life-and-death drama.

A Raw Deal

Les Francis looked at his watch; it was ten minutes past one in the afternoon. Gripping his briefcase a little tighter, he increased his step while taking a quick glance at his reflection in a store window. His grey suede jacket hung loosely on his lean tall frame and his light-brown hair was neatly groomed. His lips parted in a soft smile causing his eyes to crease at the corners. He was five minutes early for the arrival of the car that would stop outside the front gates of the city park. Les stood near the park gates and glanced again at his watch. As he did so, a young, fair-haired lady carrying a leather shoulder bag approached him and asked him the time in a soft American accent. He told her and she thanked him and took up a position a few feet away.

He coyly stole a glance in her direction as a soft summer breeze ruffled the lady's flowery dress that showed off her slim waist and long legs. Her instincts told her that he was watching her and she moved a few more yards away from him. Les moved back a bit and stood at the park entrance, waiting for his business acquaintance, Arnold Munn, to join him. He casually looked at his watch again, then along the street to see the car rounding the corner at the far end. The young lady saw it, too. She tidied her hair with her well-manicured fingers and patted her dress with the palm of her hand.

The car door opened with a soft swish and its passenger alighted. Arnold Munn turned and spoke to the driver and the car moved away. He was informally dressed in an off-white linen jacket and pants to match and wore open-toed leather sandals. He was about the same size and slightly older looking than Les and sported a thin moustache, which was the same colour as his short-cut brown hair.

The lady smiled and approached him. He greeted her with a light peck on the cheek while looking towards the park gates. On seeing Les, he raised his eyebrows. Les responded with a nod of his head before turning and entering the park. Arnold steered the lady by the elbow across the pavement, where they proceeded to follow Les through the gates. Les walked away from the park's busier main thoroughfare, which led towards the duck pond, a favourite feature in the centre of the park, and went down a less frequently used path beneath a thick canopy of trees towards an empty bench situated in dark shadow beneath an overhanging sycamore tree. He waited and felt a bit apprehensive about the young lady, who now walked beside Arnold. They stopped beside him and Arnold shook his hand and introduced them to each other.

'Les, this is Edith Perry. She is a chemist by profession and is also a dear friend of my usual partner, who couldn't come here today.'

He then turned his gaze towards Edith. 'Edith, let me introduce you to my friend and business acquaintance, Les Francis. He's in the pharmacy trade, too.'

Les forced a weak smile and briefly touched Edith's outstretched hand. He felt uneasy about the cool demeanour of this attractive female stranger who spoke with an American accent.

Arnold noticed his coldness towards her and sought to ease the tension when they were seated. He sat between them and explained the reason for Edith's presence instead of the expected male client. Les accepted his explanation and slowly relaxed. The conversation became lighter and Edith shared a joke with them. Les couldn't help noticing her even, white teeth and was taken by her clear, hazel-coloured eyes and infectious, tinkling laugh. He was completely at ease with this beautiful stranger by now.

The three were now in total harmony and Arnold felt that the time was ripe to proceed with the business. He asked Edith to hand Les a small sample from the contents in her shoulder bag. She proffered Les a small, clear plastic sachet filled with white powder. He pinched a small pinhole in it and squeezed a delicate amount onto his forefinger and rubbed it with his thumb. He then dabbed it on the back of his hand and lightly sniffed it with one nostril. The other two watched anxiously and breathed easier when he nodded his approval at its fine quality.

'When can I expect to receive the remainder, then, Miss Perry?'

'The rest of the consignment will be with you in one week's time, properly packed and ready for distribution,' she confidently assured him.

Edith returned the sachet to her bag and eased her grip on it for the first time since her arrival. Arnold nodded to Les, signalling him to give the briefcase to her, which she immediately opened. She speedily counted the bundles of used banknotes that it contained and, satisfied that all was correct, passed her shoulder bag over to Les.

The deal finalised, the three rose from the park bench and shook hands. None of them paid any heed to the bent figure of a shabbily dressed old man shuffling along the path with a small terrier on a leash until he was nearly upon them. They stood aside to let him pass, but he stopped just a few yards away. Arnold signalled for him to proceed. The old man straightened to his full height and pulled a revolver with a silencer attached from the inside of his overcoat. The three stood as if frozen to the spot; none of them spoke. The gunman motioned with the gun to Les and Arnold to sit down again. He then gestured to Edith to leave the briefcase in the centre of the path. He repeated the silent order with his gun to Les, who obediently rose from the seat and placed the shoulder bag beside the briefcase. Both he and Edith returned to the seat.

As they did so, Arnold Munn took advantage of the distraction and made a rush for the gunman, who turned swiftly towards him and fired. The silenced gunshot entered Arnold's left eye, causing him to spin round once and fall back onto the bench.

He was dead.

Les and Edith, now looking petrified, raised their hands in total surrender. The gunman moved closer and stopped a few feet from them. Les parted his lips to speak and immediately a tiny puff of smoke exited the silencer. Les slumped back on the bench and his head lolled sideward as he, too, died instantly from the missile that entered his forehead.

The gunman then returned the gun to his hidden shoulder holster and became a bent old man again. He shuffled over and lifted the briefcase. He patted his dog on the head as Edith Perry rose from the bench. She casually lifted her bag off the path and slung it from her right shoulder. Without a word, she linked her free arm in his and the two of them turned and casually left the park along with the little shaggy dog, leaving Les Francis and Arnold Munn lying dead and forgotten behind them in the park.

Con Artists

The last afternoon tour at the National Art Gallery in London was nearing an end and the group of visitors stayed close to their guide, not wanting to miss one word of his description of a painting by Pablo Picasso. It was titled *The Old Guitarist*, showing a thin, ragged, old man sitting cross-legged with his head bent, engrossed in the music that his long, bony fingers played on a Spanish guitar.

Satisfied that he had answered every question about Picasso's artwork, the guide led them to another section of the gallery. All but three of the tourists followed him. Those three stood studying the painting, making their own comments to each other about its lines and structure and seemed to be oblivious to the others moving on. It was the first time they had spoken to each other during the whole tour. One of the three men seemed to be more knowledgeable than the other two.

'You seem to know a lot about painting,' said one of the others.

'Let me introduce myself. My name is Vincent and I am a professional painter. Most people call me Vinny and I come from Holland.'

The other two introduced themselves as well. One was an electrician named Alan, who came from Wales, and the other a fitness instructor called Patrick, who was from Ireland. Patrick was on his first visit to London and it was the first time he had ever visited an art gallery.

They returned to the subject of *The Old Guitarist* again, still in no hurry to join the others, who were now in another section of the building. As they looked at the painting again, Patrick gasped in surprise. 'I'm only noticing that that picture is hanging crooked. Do any of you notice that?' he said.

Alan looked at *The Old Guitarist* painting for a few moments. 'It doesn't look too crooked to me,' he answered in a relaxed voice.

Vincent wasn't a bit perturbed either and told Patrick that the painting was level. 'You only think it is crooked because the old guitarist's head is bent. Many amateurs such as you experience optical illusions when viewing Pablo Picasso's artwork, such is the genius of the great man.'

Patrick agreed that it just might be his eyes playing tricks on him and prepared to move on to catch up with the rest of the group. Vincent asked Alan to linger another while to view some of Picasso's other paintings hanging close by and advised Patrick they would follow later.

As Patrick was moving away, the painting slipped from its supposedly horizontal position and hung at an angle as if only from one screw. Immediately, he rushed towards it, fearing that it was about to crash to the ground. Catching hold of the bottom corner of the painting, he told Alan to fetch an attendant or any of the museum officials. He then called to Vincent, who stood in shocked silence as though frozen to the spot.

'For heaven's sake, would you give yourself a shake and go as well and find somebody while I hold on to the picture.'

Vincent rushed off after Alan, leaving Patrick alone. As he stood casually looking about him, he realised that there was no-one else around. It was then that his gaze fell on a small window in a wall nearby with two double-glazed panes. He noticed that one of the panes was broken and began to feel a panic coming over him as he imagined the security guards appearing and accusing him of attempting to steal the painting.

Nervously, he called out, 'Alan, are you there?' His voice just echoed back at him. He called louder a second time, 'Alan, Vinny, where the hell have you two gotten yourselves to?' Patrick was really in a panic now and began to scream. 'I'm not going to hold this blasted picture one more minute, this skinny old bastard of a guitarist can fall and break his bloody neck as far as I'm concerned.' He listened, but nobody answered. He moved away from the picture that still hung at a precarious angle on the wall from a solitary nail.

He hadn't moved too far when he could hear garbled voices coming near and hoped that the rest of his group was returning his way. A wave of relief passed over him. The voices were getting louder now. He went to meet whoever was approaching but stopped in his tracks when he was confronted by two security guards and three museum attendants. Between them, Alan and Vincent were being frogmarched along, their wrists manacled behind their backs.

'What in heaven's name happened to you two?' Patrick asked, feeling the panic rising again. One of the guards approached him and asked him his name. Patrick told the guard who he was.

'Are you along with these two scoundrels?' the guard asked him.

Patrick's knees went weak and he answered, 'I only met them about ten minutes ago. You see, we're along with a group of visitors who are just ahead of us. We three stopped to admire that painting and when it began to hang precariously from its fixings, I sent them to find an attendant while I stayed to hold it up.'

As he spoke, the rest of the group came along and everyone went silent when they saw Alan and Vincent bound and under guard. The whole group were then taken to the security quarters and questioned about the intended theft of the Picasso painting. All were allowed to leave, except Alan and Vincent. Patrick was deemed innocent of being in on the plot to steal the famous work of art.

He later learned that the two suspects were known art thieves and had been under surveillance from the moment they had entered the museum. It was also discovered that one of them had broken the small window earlier in the day after tampering with its alarm sensor. The other had also loosened three of the picture's fixtures thus leaving it easier for them to steal the painting after the last visitors of the day had moved on but had not reckoned on it nearly falling off the wall.

'But how would they have gotten such a large picture out of such a small window?' Patrick inquired. The attendant told him that the thieves would have cut the canvas from its frame, rolled it up and just passed it out through the window to a third accomplice on the outside.

What an experience that was! Patrick thought to himself as he boarded the plane that would bring him home. *I can't wait to tell the boys at the gym about it when I get back and warn them to keep a good eye on their Picassos.*

Bumper's Confession

It was on one of those blustery, drizzly winter evenings that I was sitting at home after dinner. A Saturday it was and I needed to get out of the house or I would die with boredom after the sports had finished on TV. My wife, Sally, was content enough as she sat knitting and watching one of her favourite soaps and our 2-year-old baby, Maria, was asleep in her cot.

'I think I'll go out for a while,' I said.

'Okay, honey, watch yourself and don't be getting up to any mischief,' Sally said jokingly.

I responded by giving her a peck on the cheek, saying, 'I'm just going for a walk, sweetie, and might call in for a pint on my way home again.'

I left my house in the Creggan Estate and walked down Beechwood Avenue into the town. One hour later, I began to feel warm and thirsty and, as I neared the bottom of Bishop Street, I made up my mind to go into the Silver Dog Bar for a pint of stout.

Inside, Don the barman was polishing glasses to keep himself busy. He poured me a pint of stout and I carried it to an empty table away from the curious eyes of the handful of local old boys who lined the bar counter, engaged in whatever old men talk about. *Not too many in here for a Saturday night,* I was thinking when I was joined by a man about my own age. I surmised from the way he moved he was tipsy from over-imbibing. He introduced himself by shaking my hand.

'Hello, Tommy. It must be about four years since I last seen you,' he slurred. He seemed to be well on with the drink and I knew it would do no harm to play along with his mistaking me for someone else.

'How are you, Sammy? It must be at least three years anyway. Wasn't it in the BSR factory we worked?' I asked.

'You must be starting to dote, Tommy,' he answered in a slight English accent. 'Sure we were buddies when you, "Banty" Doyle and me worked in Morecambe Holiday Camp in England.' He lit a cigarette before continuing, 'And where did you get the Sammy from? You must be even drunker than me.' Poking his finger into my chest, he continued, 'You're Tommy "Champer" Doherty and I'm your ould buddy Barney "Bumper" Nash. Don't you remember?'

I answered with faked surprise, 'Bumper Nash? My goodness, how could I be so stupid! My ould brain isn't getting any younger, you know.' *I'll have to drink up my pint and get away from this nuisance,* I thought and swallowed the remainder of my stout quickly, then rose from my seat, telling Bumper that I must move on.

He stood up, too, and caught me firmly by the arm. 'Just you sit down there again, Champer,' he said in a raised voice with a hint of aggression. 'I only came back from England yesterday and I'm damned sure I'm not going to let my old buddy leave this bar without getting him a drink.' He then lowered his voice. 'Champer, ould buddy, I'm going to tell you about something that I have never told another living soul.'

Not wanting to make a scene in a strange bar, and knowing that everyone including the barman was now watching us, I sat down again.

Bumper continued speaking in a low voice. 'I hope you don't mind me asking, Champer, but would you sub me a drink and I'll repay you when my mate comes in? We backed a few winners today and he's away to collect our dosh.'

What the heck, I thought, *it'll do me no harm just to sit and listen to this fool and enjoy another pint of stout.* I gave him some money and he went to order the drinks.

Bumper walked unsteadily back from the bar carrying two pints of stout and, strangely enough, he didn't spill a drop, drunk and all that he seemed. He carefully set them down on the table, pulled a chair close to me and sat down. He let out a long, loud burp and looked about him, making sure that no-one could overhear before he began talking.

'Do you remember that time we worked in Morecambe and I had that wee part-time job on a Saturday, working in the bookies on the High Street?'

I nodded my head in answer and he continued.

'Well, I was running a scam along with another bloke who was working as a cashier there full time. I was writing out winners on blank dockets and cashing the dockets with him. We alternated every Saturday. It went on for almost two years and we made a small fortune. That was why, if you remember, I was able to wear those expensive suits and give you and Banty the odd fiver and no questions asked.'

I acted surprised and said, 'I always wondered about that many's the time but didn't want to be prying into your affairs and that's why I never asked any questions.'

Bumper continued with what seemed to be a confession to me. 'When you went back home to Derry, I got Banty a part-time job in the same bookies at the weekends. I couldn't let him in on the scam, though, because my other bookie colleague warned me on peril of my life not to let anyone else know what we were up to.'

'You were getting in very deep, then?' I asked, keeping up my pretence.

'You're damned right I was. We had so much money that I was putting it into a safe-deposit box and I was still giving Banty the odd fiver as well. Then, one day, the police arrived and took my partner and me into the back office. They asked us if we knew anything about any punters cashing dodgy betting dockets. Of course, we denied ever knowing anything about them.' He took a sip of stout and wiped the foam from his lips and continued his story. 'The boss kept a close watch on everything from then on. Boy, was I sweating. We would have been in major bother if my partner hadn't thought up a plan to get the boss from looking over our shoulders. He framed Banty by planting a fraudulent docket in his coat pocket and letting him cash it. Banty was caught in the act and taken away by the police, who were keeping a close eye on things.' Bumper shook his head as he finished his story. 'Poor ould Banty Doyle was imprisoned for three years and we got off scot-free.'

I was really flabbergasted by his story. 'You are a very clever fellow, Bumper,' I lied and thought, *What a rotten sod he must be to let his closest buddy go to jail! I'm glad I never knew the creep before.*

Bumper drained his glass and rose from the table. He stood swaying. 'I'm afraid I'll have to tap you again for another pint, Champer. As you can see, my friend hasn't turned up yet.'

'You just sit down there again, Bumper, and I will bring you one,' I lied, thinking, *The moment I get near that door, I'm getting to feck out of this madhouse.*

Nearing the door, the huge bulk of a man I didn't know blocked my path. 'You going home, pal?' he asked.

I was scared as I answered, 'I was going to go earlier, but Bumper over there asked me to get him another drink.'

'Did he tell you anything about working in a bookmaker's shop in England?' the stranger asked.

'Something like that,' I answered, 'but I didn't believe him. He also told me that he and some other guy who worked in the bookies had some sort of a scam going, cashing false betting dockets, and that some other guy called Banty Doyle, who was supposed to be his buddy, took the rap for it. It sounded too far-fetched for me. And another thing, he has already tapped me for two pints and that's why I'm getting out of here.'

The big man's eyes narrowed and he breathed slowly and heavily as he tightened his fists and jaws. *This other nut bin is going to give me a hiding for nothing,* I thought, and was preparing to make a break for the door when he grasped my hand and shook it. Relief flooded through me.

'Thanks, pal,' he growled through clenched teeth. 'Just you go on home and I'll deal with that scumbag Mr Barney Bumper Nash.'

Then, before leaving, I nervously asked him his name. He turned his eyes towards Bumper before answering, 'I'm Banty Doyle's brother.'

I hurried away from the door of the Silver Dog as fast as my shaking legs would carry me, the sweat now beginning to feel cool on my forehead with the late evening air. After walking to the bottom of Bishop Street, I turned the corner into Hamilton Street and gave a little hop and jump and punched the air with delight. I hurried back to my happy home and family, satisfied that long-overdue justice was about to come crashing down on a nasty piece of work who richly deserved it.

One Man and His Dog

The river had risen with the heavy rain during the night and was just perfect for the trout and salmon to ascend the steep rock face into their first resting pool. I was feeling pleased at having arrived early before the invasion of a host of other equally excited anglers. Standing at the edge of the river on the High Bank, I cast my line, rested the tip of the rod on a forked stick and sat on my stool waiting patiently for a bite. A loud, heavy splash below the carry made my nerves jump. *A large trout or a grilse; the fish must be on the move,* I thought, keeping my eye on the line.

The pained yelping of a dog and someone cursing, followed by another heavy splash a few yards away, caused me to rise and move back onto the river path to investigate what was happening. I could see no movement, although I heard a man swearing angrily. 'You're only good for wolfing down food and lying across the front doormat, you rotten, lazy cur.'

Feeling concerned, I walked down the path and stopped abruptly when I observed Mickey Tam, a tall, thin elderly bachelor from the village, kicking a soaking-wet Golden Labrador back down the bank into the water from where it had scrambled. A piece of rope with a brick tied to it hung from its neck.

'Are you having a bit of bother, Mickey?' I asked, causing him to turn quickly and stare at me with surprise and guilt.

'I … I didn't think anyone else was about at this time of the morning. Sorry if I disturbed you,' he mumbled back.

I asked him what was happening with the dog. 'It's such an ould brute of a coward and a useless grub destroyer as well,' he answered. 'My house was broken into last night and after I chased the thief away, I found that lily-livered excuse of a dog shivering with fear under the kitchen table and now I'm drowning it.'

As he spoke, the dog scrambled from the river again, ran towards me and sat whimpering and shivering against my leg. I took the rope from its neck and it licked my hand in gratitude. Mickey, who by now seemed angrier than ever, grabbed it by the scruff of its neck, causing it to yelp again with fright.

He was about to throw it back into the river when he lost his footing, fell backwards into the water and was carried away with the current. I ran along the bank and watched him flailing his arms about as he floated under the overhanging branches of a willow tree. It was then that the Labrador immediately bounded into the water and swam along with the flow to catch up with Mickey, who was by now calling for help and hanging by one hand to the tip of one of the branches. As the Labrador neared him, he lost his grip and went under for a few seconds only to surface again a few yards further downstream. The dog swam along with the fast current and tried to catch the tails of his coat that were floating on top of the water behind him. It managed to grasp one end of the coattail, but Mickey was struggling so much that his coat slipped again from the dog's mouth. The Labrador seemed to gain extra strength and, in one great effort, swam closer and caught Mickey's coat collar in its jaws and swam with its floundering master to a shallower part of the river, where I was able to wade out and drag him to safety.

Mickey lay there gasping on the grass and the Labrador was whimpering and began to lick his face. He put his arms around its neck, crying, 'Thank you, thank you, my ever-faithful friend,' he sobbed. 'I will never try to hurt you again.' His Labrador yelped happily and began licking the streaming hot tears from its master's cheeks.

I must admit that I shed a little tear of happiness for them both that day and that incident returns fresh to my mind each time I see Mickey Tam walking through the village with his faithful Golden Labrador close by his side.

Brief Encounter

Greg McCaul parked his car and leisurely walked towards the entrance to the supermarket. He was going through his memorised shopping list: bread, easy-spread butter, milk, cheddar cheese, full-cream milk and a punnet of strawberries. The angel-sweet voice of his bride-to-be one week from now still lingered in his ear. 'And don't forget the tea bags, darling. They must be Punjana only and nothing else.'

He himself had added another item to the list. *I'll surprise her with a bunch of flowers as well; she would like that,* he thought. Collecting a basket, he wove his way between slow-moving shoppers and stationary trolleys towards the bakery counter, where he picked up a newly baked French long loaf. He then made his way to the dairy shelves, where he moved carefully along looking at the various products in search of the fresh cream. He was abruptly stopped in his tracks on receiving a painful blow to his buttocks from a moving shopping trolley. He winced and turned sharply to remonstrate with the offender but before he could express his annoyance, the owner of the trolley began apologising profusely. It was a young lady in her late twenties.

'Please forgive me, sir, I hope I haven't injured you. I should have been more careful, but my mind was somewhere else and I didn't notice you.' Her cheeks were coloured a deep pink with embarrassment.

Greg forgave her instantly when he felt the sincerity of her apology. 'I'm quite fine,' he said, smiling. 'I was just startled because I was so immersed in my shopping. Don't worry about it, it could happen to anybody.'

The young lady smiled and asked him if he needed any help. Greg, knowing that she was attempting to make up for her careless trolley driving and not wanting to reject her gesture, said that he would be grateful if she could help him to find the fresh cream. She brushed close to him as she reached her hand to a lower shelf in the cabinet and retrieved a tub of fresh dairy cream. Greg caught the pleasant fragrance from her and couldn't help admiring the highlights in the silkiness of her long red hair, which was tied in a ponytail. He thanked her and placed the cream into his basket, then held out his open hand towards her. 'I'm Greg McCaul.'

The young lady responded by gently shaking hands. 'I'm very pleased to meet you, Greg. My name is Sharon Delaney, *Miss* Sharon Delaney, that is. Do you shop here often?' she inquired, more to strike up a casual conversation than wanting to pry into his shopping habits.

Greg told her that he didn't shop for groceries too often and that when he came to that particular supermarket he usually had a cup of coffee in the cafeteria. 'I just have to get a bunch of flowers first,' he said. 'Would you like to join me, Miss Delaney … that is, if you are nearly done with your shopping?'

Sharon said that she had one or two more items to get first and she would meet him in the cafeteria for a nice cup of tea and a pastry in a few minutes. Her cheeks took on a deep-pinkish glow again when Greg said that he would have a cup waiting for her. *What a nice, well-mannered, friendly girl,* he thought, rubbing a still-tingling buttock as he moved towards the cafeteria.

Sharon was thinking, *What a lovely gentleman, and quite handsome, too. It's a wonder I've never noticed him in here before. The flowers must be for his mother.* She joined him in the cafeteria and they were soon exchanging niceties about their jobs and pastimes and musical interests. Sharon went slightly further when she asked Greg if he had a girlfriend. She seemed slightly deflated when she learned that he was going to marry his beautiful fiancée in one week's time.

'I had been married at one time at a very young age,' she told him, 'but I parted company with my unfaithful husband when the stars had cleared from my eyes and I eventually came down to earth again. In other words, our honeymoon had ended sooner than planned.'

'I'm sorry to hear that, Sharon, but you are still quite a very attractive young lady and I'm sure you won't be alone for very long, as there is more than one fish in the sea.'

The conversation drifted again and Sharon cut her pastry in halves. She offered one of them to Greg, who gratefully accepted and began nibbling it as they chatted away. Half an hour had passed and he looked at his watch. 'Gee! Look at the time, Miss Delaney,' he said with surprise. 'It's time I was getting back to my flat or my girlfriend will think that something has happened to me.'

Sharon acted surprised as well. 'Doesn't time fly when one is in nice company!' Rising from her seat, she extended her dainty hand. 'Thank you for the tea and your pleasant company, Greg. Please accept my best wishes and happiness to you and your fiancée on your wedding day.'

Greg, who was already standing, shook her hand, thanked her and walked away.

Sharon watched him leave the cafeteria and gave a deep sigh as she whispered, 'What a lucky woman who will soon be married to that man in a million.'

She sighed again and proceeded to push her trolley in the direction of the car park. Sharon started to make her way to her car but was impeded by a small group of people who seemed to be gathered around the prone figure of a man on the ground. She made her way round them and then, as she glanced sideward, she heard her name being uttered, 'Sharon, Sharon.'

Sharon recognised the voice and pushed her way through to see Greg on the ground clutching a bunch of yellow roses. 'I know this man; his name is Greg McCaul and he is calling for me. I was talking to him just a minute or two ago in the cafeteria.' She knelt by Greg's side and whispered into his ear, 'What happened to you, Greg?'

Greg answered her weakly. 'I was putting my shopping into my car and felt very dizzy. I think it was that piece of pastry I ate; there must have been something in it. Would you know if there was any trace of almonds in it? You see, I'm allergic to them and I could die if I don't get to a hospital immediately.'

Sharon gasped and jumped to her feet. 'Oh, my God, the pastry was marzipan flavoured and it's my favourite pastry.' The car park attendant, who was on his knees beside Greg, heard their every word and rushed to his office and called for an ambulance, which arrived within five minutes.

Sharon Delaney never saw Greg again, even though she looked out for him in the supermarket every time she shopped there. At times, she felt her heart skip a beat when she thought she saw him reaching into the dairy-food cabinet only to feel a great disappointment in discovering that her imagination had only been playing tricks on her.

As it turned out, it was better for Sharon that she still felt that romantic yearning to meet Greg McCaul again than to learn that by the time he arrived at the hospital he was in a deep coma and died twenty minutes later after that first and last brief encounter.

Bolshie Babies

One of the sweetest sounds that we often hear has to be the noises and giggles and gurgles that babies utter during their first months on this planet. This tinkling, gaga sound is said to be just innocent baby talk. That's what I always believed until an experience I had not so many years ago made me think otherwise.

When I was employed as an assistant groundsman in Brooke Park, I remember I was working around the flowerbeds and stopped to take my morning break. I sat on a bench and lit up a cigarette before opening my newspaper. In the meantime, four young ladies pushing prams came along the main path and sat down on the bench next to mine. The babies were all about six or seven months old and I presumed the women were the babies' mothers.

The mothers knew each other and were soon immersed in conversation about their wee weans. 'My Lisa is an ould granny,' and 'my wee Colin is going to be a footballer when he grows up,' and 'our big dote Ben is cutting a tooth and slabbering profusely.'

That was how the general conversation flowed. One mum talked about how intelligent and advanced her wee darling, John, was and how he just loves watching *Big*

Brother and that he was now able to say Da-da and Ma-ma and wa-wa and ga-ga and that he was now eating bits of grilled sausages and Doherty's mince. Another was excitedly telling the rest that her wee boy could devour a full round of bread soaked in tea inside a couple of minutes and would eat more if he were given it.

One of the mothers had a large blanket with her, which she spread out on the grass, and the four babies were set down on it and given their soft toys, rattles, teddies, teething rings and the like to keep themselves amused. The four ladies were chatting and chittering away at ten to the dozen as I browsed through my paper. The weans who were also chatting baby talk among themselves as they pulled and hauled at each other's toys.

I was happily drifting into my own world when I noticed the little voices began to intrude into my senses and distract my reading. I gradually got attuned to their rhythm and I was mysteriously able to understand their every word. I could hardly believe my own ears and pretended to read my newspaper as I listened in amazement to their patter.

'Are you still on the organic milk, Ben?' asked Lisa.

'Aye. Just in the mornings, Lisa,' replied Ben. 'In the evenings and at night, I get formula.'

'What about you, Colin?' she inquired. 'Still on the organic or have you been upgraded to Cow and Gate?'

Colin shook his rattle in frustration as he answered. 'I was on full cream until the shenanigans of our milkman.'

'Why was that, then, Colin?' she asked.

'It's a long story, I'll tell you about it some other time. But I had to be fed with Farley's rusks and water to satisfy my hunger after that carry on.'

'Lousy so-and-so,' said John, who was the smallest of the four and who had been contentedly sitting sucking his thumb. 'And what does your dad say about it?' he asked.

'I don't remember ever having had a dad,' replied Colin, 'but I heard my granny saying that I resembled the milkman.'

Lisa took up the lead again. 'Mmm, he could be your da, all right.'

John spoke again, a touch of anger in his tone. 'Do youse know what? My da comes home with a few drinks in him every Friday night and he brings a feed of chips and chicken curry with him and him and my ma eats it after I'm put into my cot. And do youse know what else? See when my ma gives me a feed in the middle of the night, my mouth beez burning with the taste of that curry she ate and I scream my head off until I get bottled milk.'

I couldn't believe what I was hearing from those four babies, and not one of them even a year old yet!

Baby Lisa carried on the conversation.

'I never have had any bother with my food ever since my mum took me off the organic milk a month ago because it was giving me a rash on my bottom. I had to have lots of cream plastered on after every feed, and now that I'm on a daily diet of goat's milk, my skin is as clear and smooth as my granda's baldy head again.'

Ben began slapping a teddy bear about the face. 'I'm fed up being treated like a lodger and am going to start protesting about not getting any Farley's rusks or curried milk like youse uns.' He threw his teddy bear aside and punched the air with his tiny fist. 'In fact, I'm going to demand that we get our own goat.'

Colin agreed angrily. 'I'm going to protest as well about not getting my fair share of the organic milk.'

John immediately joined in with his complaint. 'Youse have every right to protest, and I am going to join with youse and shout about having to drink that ould, rotten bottled milk. I would rather have Cow and Gate instead of that watery crap.'

I was smiling now as their talk became more aggressive and listened more carefully to hear Lisa suggesting that they begin an immediate protest to their mums about the unsatisfactory state of affairs concerning their feeds.

'Right,' she ordered, 'we are going to kick up the greatest mother of stinks right here and now until our demands are met. Now, on the count of three, we will start wailing as loud as we can. One, two, and three …'

The four babies started screaming their heads off and lay on their backs, kicking their legs about as if they were being stung by a swarm of bees. I had to put my hands over my ears, the noise was so loud, and their shocked mothers rushed to them and lifted them to soothe their cries. But the screaming continued as the babies were returned to their prams and hurriedly wheeled out of the park.

I returned to my work in the flowerbed while in the distance could still be heard the loud protesting cries of the four little babies.

She

Strangers we sheltered
From a summer rain
Bodies huddled close
Warm and moist
Beneath her parasol
Strangers we parted
Now she pervades my dreams
The pale hazel pools in her eyes
Ripples my being
I catch my breath
To linger long
In a fraction
Of a moment
Her woman fragrance
Exciting my soul
My mind
My senses
My desires
Her satin-soft skin
Warm
Against my heart

Those pale hazel pools
Subduing
Caressing
Embalming
Willing me to savour
To imbibe
To succumb
To surrender
To love

Different Paths

The other day, I was looking through an old, yellowing *Derry Journal* that had been used as a drawer liner when I came across the Twenty-Years-Ago page. There were four pictures in it and one of them caught my attention. It was taken at a school sports prizegiving ceremony and included myself along with four of my Christian Brothers Technical School companions during the 1950s. It got me thinking back over the years, remembering the paths our lives had taken since that pleasant day.

The first boy was called Eddie Kearney. He was a stocky, broad-shouldered, black-haired lad who lived at the top of the Bogside near the city abattoir that was then better known locally as the slaughterhouse. He loved taking part in all kinds of sports; soccer being his first preference, with Gaelic football coming next. He was always in the forefront at the school sports events such as pole vaulting, high jumping, running and javelin throwing.

Eddie didn't do too well in the classroom, though, being punished at least twice every week for his untidy approach and sometimes not having done his homework. His excuse was that his little 3-year-old brother was always taking out his books and tearing out the homework pages. The teacher knew differently, suspecting that Eddie played so much football after school in the street or in Meenan Park that he never went home until it was near his bedtime.

Eddie finally said farewell to his schooldays when he turned sixteen and played in numerous junior soccer teams in the city until he was spotted by a scout from one of the senior English teams and left Derry to train for Newcastle United. It was there that he honed his football skills until he secured his place on the first team. After three years away, he became homesick, returned to Derry, and was asked to sign up by Derry City Football Club. As a left-winger, Eddie was a great strength to his side, scoring on numerous occasions, and was instrumental in them winning four finals in Windsor Park.

His soccer days over, Eddie took up employment in one of the local engineering factories until his death from throat cancer in his fifties. A sad end it was to one of my dearest old school friends and one of Derry City's best football players.

Next in the photo was Oscar Ensley, who lived in Barry Street. He was the complete opposite of Eddie. Slender and gentle mannered, he shied away from all physical-contact activities. His reason for being in the photograph was that he handed the prizes to the schoolteacher as he presented them to the winners. He sang in the school choir and solo in the Our Boys concerts that were staged each year in St Columb's Hall to packed houses. At the annual Derry Feis, Oscar did the school proud by winning many solos and choir competitions. He was also a very keen Irish step-dancer, and at that, too, he brought many honours to Nellie Sweeney's dancing school by collecting his fair share of the trophies and medals. I don't remember him ever being late or absent for school or ever being punished with the leather strap.

Beside Oscar in the picture was Denis Cassidy, who was a head boy and very much respected by everyone at the school until he left at eighteen. He went to live with relations in London and got into acting, taking part in local drama groups. Gaining confidence and experience, Denis obtained parts in a few minor Pinewood Studio films until his big break came at thirty-five and he got main acting roles in some of the B movies.

I still see Denis now and then on TV and in the odd film and met him only last year when he was in Donegal with a film crew. It wasn't by coincidence, either, that we met, because he contacted me a few weeks before coming to Ireland and arranged for me to stay with him and the crew for a couple of days. I couldn't believe that I had once sat beside this blossoming film actor when I went to school. That was my nearest encounter to fame. Denis is now about to retire and is living in California. We haven't contacted each other for the past number of years, but, God willing, we will meet again one day.

My next school associate in the photograph was Harry Piggott from Rossville Street. He was a popular and likeable character, one of those cool, streetwise types that everyone liked to hang around with in the schoolyard and whom bullies avoided.

An above-average scholar, he always seemed to exist somewhere in the middle of the spectrum, keeping his head down to escape any unsavoury attention from the teachers. Harry Piggott was always the one for pulling pranks on the less wary classmates and getting away with them because of his ability to laugh and to show that there was never any malice in his actions.

On school sports days, he was always sure to win prizes and we somehow knew that he cheated a little now and then or bribed some of the other boys to let him come in first, second or third place. Being a fair footballer, too, Harry just about did enough in every contest to justify his getting a permanent place on the school team. One thing I envied him for, though, was that he was never selected to sing in the school choir or 'action' songs at the annual Derry Feis. I could never escape the test and hadn't the courage to sing off key, as Harry always did, to get rejected from any and all school music activities.

I never remember Harry ever getting into trouble and never heard him speaking ill about anybody, not even about some of the biggest-known sneaks at the school. He went through his school days happy and contented without even faking being sick or playing truant like the rest of us. He was a truly sound person of honourable traits that anybody would have been pleased to include in their circle of friends.

Harry left the Christian Brothers at sixteen and found employment with one of the local building contractors, where he stayed until he was nineteen. Work being scarce in Derry at the time, Harry went to London to work on the building sites and soon was promoted to general manager. He came back every now and then to visit his family and to renew old friendships. It was on one of those visits I had a conversation with him about his personal life in London. He owned his own apartment in Putney and had a few short romantic relationships over the years that ended amiably. Marriage was at the bottom of his priorities and I could understand that, knowing that Harry was never one to jump into any situation feet first. He still remained as cool and streetwise as he had been in his schooldays.

Over the years, I lost all contact with Harry until a friend who had worked along with him in London came back to live in Derry again. He told me that Harry had eventually met and married a lovely, fair-haired London girl. One year after they were married, she had a child and Harry went to visit her and his new baby boy at the hospital. His world fell apart that day when his wife tearfully admitted that the baby was not his.

Harry could not cope with this revelation. Soon after, he left her and the child and London itself far behind. The last thing I heard about Harry was that he had been living rough in Birmingham, going from job to job and drinking heavily. His family in Derry gradually lost track of him and haven't heard anything about him since.

As for myself being the fifth person in the school photograph, I have survived here in Derry until now, and think often about all of my other school friends in my quiet moments, not forgetting to say a wee prayer now and then for Harry Piggott.

Nightmare in the Barber's Shop

'The usual, Phil?' – his customary greeting.

'Aye, just the usual, Cyril, and I'll have a shave as well,' I replied as I sat comfortably in the barber's chair, lifting my chin to let him tuck the cloth over my shirt collar.

Cyril was elderly and long past the retirement age for most men. Being one of the oldest hairdressers in the business, he conveyed a deep knowledge of any topic – from sport and world politics to religion, aviation and gardening, even though, to the best of my knowledge, he had never been a priest, worked in a garden or flew in an aeroplane in all his long life. Or barely left Derry for that matter. I happened to be his last client for the day, it being a Wednesday and the only day of the week that the shop closed at five o'clock.

'Not at work today, then, Phil?' he asked in an unconcerned tone as if he couldn't care less, his mind on something else.

He began to cut the back of my hair as I replied, 'Naw, sure I couldn't face work this morning after lying awake all night with a sore throat. Every swallow I took felt as if strands of barbed wire were being pulled into my gullet.'

Cyril was using the clippers now on the sides of my temples and would soon use them to tidy up the back of my head. He finished the finer shaping of my hair and fetched the soaping mug and wobbling brush. He then busied himself, holding a small towel under the hot water before wringing it out and dabbing it on the stubble on my face. After he soaped me, he wiped his hands on his white apron, saying, 'I have to nip into the bookies next door to see the racing results. I backed the last two favourites.' At the door, he called back to me, 'Stall there till I get back and that beard will be right and soft and easier to shave.'

'I'll be here, all right,' I replied, eyeing him through the mirror. 'Hope your horses come up.'

I sat twiddling my thumbs and looking about the shelves whereon sat an array of bottles of different-coloured liquids and an assortment of soaps and powders. Now and then, I smiled at my reflection sporting the white foam beard that looked back at me from the huge mirror. The peaceful silence and slow ticking from a clock in the shop was beginning to lull me into a relaxing, drowsy mood and I felt my soft, rhythmic breathing, which made my eyelids feel heavy.

They were just about to close when a mouse scurried from behind a waste bin to examine a small bit of debris that lay a couple of inches away from a brush standing against the wall. The wee timid creature quickly retreated again when I moved my foot and only the muffled sounds of street noises drifted through the slightly open door. I was breathing very slowly now, deep and heavy until I began to drift off, the loss of sleep the previous night now taking its toll.

My chair began to float and I felt myself swaying with its gentle motion. The mouse appeared again from somewhere and sat on my knee on its hind legs, moistening its little forepaws with its tongue, then rubbing them about its head and behind its ears. It was washing itself and now and then looking up into my face and I thought that it was the cutest little creature I had ever seen, with its little whiskers twitching and its round, languid, childlike eyes looking deeply into mine.

I was transfixed until it began to grow larger and take on a wolfish appearance. Becoming frightened, I didn't dare move for fear it would spring at my throat, which was starting to feel jagged again. I felt feverish now with terror and suddenly the creature screamed and brought me to my senses.

Cyril was sharpening the razor on the broad leather strap that hung from a hook on the wall. 'I must have dozed off and didn't hear you coming back,' I said in relief. 'I imagined that there was a mouse sitting on my knee and it turned into a wolf and started screaming at me.'

He didn't laugh as I had expected him to but said nothing as he finished sharpening his razor and examining its gleaming blade. Rubbing a finger across its edge and then holding it in front of his face, he turned to me. I sat motionless as he started to shout in rage as he moved towards me. It must have been his loud screams earlier that had woken me and I gripped the arms of the chair, not knowing what was happening. Cyril stood in front of me, holding the razor above my head like an axe that was about to split a block of wood. His eyes were staring wildly, like a terrified animal, not *at* me, but *through* me as if I weren't in his presence, as though he were in a trance. I was frozen to the chair, not knowing what had come over him.

'What's wrong, Cyril?' I croaked, 'did anything happen to you in the bookies?'

He swiped the razor above my head.

'Bookies? Is that what you call them?' he shouted back at me, his eyes now staring wildly into my face. 'They're robbing, fecking bastards, that's what they are. And if I had my way, I'd cut all their fecking throats.'

As he said it, he swiped the gleaming razor through the air in front of my face. I realised then that Cyril's horses must have been beaten and that he must have lost a fair amount of money on them. I was about to ask him how his bet went when he moved towards me and placed his left hand heavily on my chest. The glinting razor was in the other hand and he placed it against my throat. His breathing was fast and warm on my face, but I dared not move a muscle, fearing that he would pull the lethal instrument across my thrapple. *I won't have to worry about swallowing barbed wire ever again,* I thought.

'Is your throat still sore, Phil?' he whispered as he scraped the razor up along my windpipe, removing the foam and stubble and wiping it off on a piece of tissue paper. I swallowed hard, feeling my Adam's apple rise and fall before quivering forth an answer.

'It's not too bad now, Cyril.'

He was breathing lighter now.

'That's good, Phil, and it'll feel even better when I'm finished with you.'

I didn't say anything but began inwardly saying an act of contrition as he continued to shave me with long, confident, accurate strokes.

His mood suddenly changed and he became quieter and more relaxed. 'I'm sorry for my outburst,' he said, 'but I was very annoyed at losing my bet. I was so sure that I would make a rise, but I'll make it up again soon.'

Joyous relief slowly spread through me. 'That's all right, Cyril,' I croaked. 'You probably were disappointed, and nobody likes to lose on the favourites.'

The agony was over when Cyril wiped my face with a clean towel. Releasing me from the chair, he asked, 'Need anything for the weekend?'

'No, thanks, Cyril,' I answered and paid him before briskly making for the door. Having reached relative safety, I stopped and turned to say, 'I'll see you again sometime, Cyril.' But in my mind I was saying, *Never again. I think it's about time you retired and went to see a good psychiatrist.*

I closed the door behind me and in utter relief deeply breathed in huge gulps of pure, clean, fresh air, feeling thankful that I had survived the Demon Barber and my throat was still in one working piece.

The Face in the Mirror

It happened years ago when I was a single, innocent, teenager. I had gone to meet some of my pals in the Forrester's snooker hall in Magazine Street and then went with them to Tracey's Bar in William Street for a wee bottle of stout. When the bar closed as usual at ten o'clock, I left my friends and made my way home to Creggan Estate.

On the way I met a girl I'd never laid eyes on before and we got into conversation. She introduced herself as Maria and told me she was an Italian student from Sorrento and was staying with some other foreign students in a rented house in Beechwood Avenue.

We chatted mostly about the changeable Irish weather and of how it differed from the sunny climate she was used to back in Sorrento. Maria was beautiful and her angel voice as she spoke in broken English sounded like heavenly music. I was slowly falling for her, even though I had only met her a few minutes earlier, and was head over heels in love by the time she stopped at the front door of her lodgings in Beechwood Avenue and invited me in for a cup of coffee. I hastily agreed and floated on a cloud behind her as we entered.

Once inside, my thoughts of romance were rudely interrupted by the sound of loud music and happy voices coming from the back of the house. 'What's going on in here, then?' I asked.

She looked into my eyes and smiled, showing her perfectly even, gleaming white teeth.

'Oh, we have a little party now and then when it's someone's birthday, and tonight it's Fred's party. He's an English boy and he is twenty today.'

I followed her into a room full of dancing, laughing young men and women and immediately a drink was put into my hand; it tasted like vodka and orange and it was pleasantly palatable.

I must have been at the party for about two hours and Maria never left my side, drinking and dancing with me the whole time until the music ended. Then, one by one and two by two, the students began drifting away to other parts of the house leaving only Maria and me embracing in the middle of the room. My head was spinning and we sat down on the settee.

'I should lie down for a while, Maria,' I slurred as she kissed me over and over again. I was so happy and giddy as I stretched out on the settee with Maria lying beside me, her head resting on my chest until both of us fell asleep.

***

The house was silent when I awoke alone early in the morning. Maria must have gone to her room sometime during the night. My mouth felt like the inside of a fur boot and a brass band was playing inside my head. I was shivering and needed to go to the bathroom which I found at the far end of a large kitchen. I quietly went in and locked the door. After relieving myself, I turned on the tap over the wash-hand basin to splash some cold water on my face. I drank some of the cool, refreshing liquid from my cupped hands and looked in the mirror to see if my eyes were still in their right sockets. 'Holy Jeez!' I wailed when I saw the terrible vision that was looking back at me. I rubbed my eyes and looked again. It was still there, only this time it was worse as it opened its mouth at the same time as I did to utter curses of shock and horror. It was then I realised that the face in the mirror that mocked and mimicked my every movement was the reflection of my own.

'Holy God Almighty! What in the blazes has happened to me?'

I moaned as I felt for my hair and eyebrows that had been completely shaved off and replaced with black and red indelible ink. And someone had painted a Hitler-like moustache above my upper lip.

I frantically rubbed my face with soap and water to try to remove the pen marks without even a tiny hint of success. The only thing I could do now was to dry myself and make my way home without meeting anyone. But first of all, I wanted to say goodbye to my lovely Maria and make a date to see her again when my hair and eyebrows grew back again.

I ascended the stairs and peeped into every bedroom until I found her sleeping fully dressed on top of her bed. I crept over to give her a goodbye peck on the cheek and screamed inside my aching brain when I beheld the face of my once lovely Maria. She'd also had her eyebrows removed and had false spectacles drawn around her lovely eyes. Thank goodness the perpetrators of the sick prank had spared her beautiful dark hair.

I made to leave her bedroom when she awoke. Seeing me, she emitted a high, piercing scream in Italian at the top of her voice. There was no time to stop and convince her that the weird looking creature now standing in her bedroom was me, so I took to my heels and rushed down the stairs.

I pulled up the collar of my jacket and dodged quickly out the front door to hopefully slip home without being noticed. The world just wasn't ready to witness such a horrible sight so early in the morning.

Finger of Fate

It was 8.30 in the morning and Pat McCartney was in a very grumpy mood as he sat in his car at the taxi rank in Foyle Street waiting for his first fare of the day. He hadn't had a good night's sleep with his new-born twin boys keeping him and his wife up most of the night with their crying.

Why do weans have to cry at night? he thought. *You would think they were doing it for pure spite. She's just as bad, too, sticking up for them and telling me that they're teething.* He yawned. *I hope to God I don't get some ould awkward customer this morning or I'll crack up.*

Just then, a voice on his radio disturbed his thoughts.

'Pat, would you pick up a fare in Wellington Street? It's some ould doll and she seems to be doting or something.'

Pat moved off. 'That's all I need this morning,' he grumbled.

He drove to the address and went to the door, thinking, *If she gives me any bother, I'll tell her to phone another taxi service.*

Pat lifted the shining brass knocker and rapped extra loudly on the door. From inside came the frail, thin voice of an old woman. 'Hold on a wee minute, please.'

Then he heard something heavy being dragged along the hallway.

What the hell is she up to?

The door opened and the small face of a woman of about eighty years or more looked up at him. 'Good morning, young man,' she said and asked him to carry her battered old suitcase to the car. 'I'm so sorry for keeping you waiting,' she said meekly.

Pat put the case into the boot and then helped her into the back seat and got in behind the steering wheel. 'Where to?' he abruptly asked as he moved off.

The old woman gave him an address and, looking at her through the rear-view mirror, Pat could see her eyes filled with tears. 'Could you take me through the town centre?' she asked.

'It's not the shortest way,' he answered.

'I don't mind, I'll pay for the extra time,' she said. 'You see, I'm going to the hospice to live so I've got plenty of time and I've got no family left in Derry or anywhere else.'

Pat looked in the mirror again and the tears were running down her wrinkled face. He drove her around the town centre and she pointed out to where the Corinthian Ballroom had once stood.

'That's where I first met my husband,' she told him. 'And there's the insurance office I once worked in,' she went on, pointing to another building. She showed him the upstairs flat she and her husband had shared after they were married and where the dressmaking shop once stood where she got her wedding dress. The old woman asked Pat to stop at a number of various other places, where she just sat for a few minutes looking out at the buildings in silence, her mind elsewhere. Pat was by now feeling pangs of guilt and sympathy for being so critical of her earlier and turned off his meter discreetly.

Much later, they arrived at the hospice and Pat carried the old woman's case as she hobbled along beside him, leaning on his arm. He accompanied her to the reception desk, where she was welcomed and asked to sign in. He could feel the moisture welling in his eyes as she kissed him gently on the cheek. 'Goodbye, you lovely gentleman, thanks for the company,' were her last words to him before being escorted through large double-doors to the heart of the building.

Pat left her there with a feeling of sadness in his heart. He also felt the moisture glistening in his eyes while his mind was deep in thought about the gentle old woman's situation. He felt guilty about his selfish behaviour when he first arrived at her front door earlier that morning.

Sitting back at the taxi rank again, he quietly said, 'I've got a lot to be thankful for. I have a lovely wife and two beautiful baby boys, and I'm sure that the finger of fate has brought me and that sweet old lady together this morning.'

When Pat McCartney arrived home that evening, he hugged his wife and told her that he had had one of the most important and meaningful days of his life. She looked at him strangely, uncertain as to what had brought on this unusual bout of emotion but content that their future was going to be long and secure together.

Dodgy Dealings on the Buncrana Bus

Frank O'Loan, a well-dressed, middle-aged, plump man with a reddish complexion, alighted in a hurry from the taxi that had brought him to the Lough Swilly bus stop in Derry's Patrick Street. Having paid his fare, he rushed to the rear of the vehicle to retrieve a bulky brown suitcase from the boot before the driver could assist him. The bus to Buncrana was about to leave and he beckoned to its driver to open the luggage compartment door. He was breathless by the time he had loaded his heavy suitcase and boarded.

O'Loan made his way to the only empty window seat, halfway down the bus. He mopped his forehead with a handkerchief and exhaled a long, loud breath of relief and loosened his tie.

As the bus moved off, he settled down, opened his newspaper and began to read. A few minutes into the journey, a bespectacled, bony-faced young lady wearing a grey tracksuit with 'Hollywood' emblazoned across her chest and a white baseball cap with a Brad Pitt motif on its peak interrupted him with a light tap on the shoulder. He turned to look at her, annoyance written on his face. *Obviously, an avid cinema enthusiast,* he thought.

'Excuse me,' she said, chewing gum at the same

time, 'is there any chance of you letting me have the entertainments section from your paper? I want to see if George Clooney's latest movie is showing in Buncrana.'

O'Loan turned his head, tensed his lips and narrowed his eyes.

'If you don't mind, young lady, I don't like being disturbed when I'm reading my newspaper.' He snapped his paper and resumed reading.

The film addict rolled her eyes, cracked a gum bubble towards his ear and sat back again, muttering, 'Bloody selfish banker.'

Overhearing her remark, he slowly lowered his newspaper. He turned his head and looked at her through the gap between the seats.

'Excuse me, young lady,' he said more timidly now, 'but do I know you?'

She cracked another gum bubble before replying, 'No, but I know you. I saw you before in the Northern Bank in Derry. I used to have an account there and you were behind the counter.'

O'Loan was more humble now and thought it better not to continue the conversation. He poked the newspaper through the gap, saying, 'Forgive me for being so abrupt, but I don't feel the best today.' He wiggled the paper. 'Here, you can have this while I take a little nap.'

The film addict took the paper and sat back contentedly in her seat again to open the entertainments pages. Just at that, she heard someone giggling and turned her gaze across the aisle to see a middle-aged man wearing an Australian bush hat, looking down towards his feet. He was still giggling as he turned to meet her gaze. 'G'day,' he said in a strong Australian accent.

'Hi, there, Crocodile Dundee,' she replied in a

fake Australian accent. 'Do you mind turning your kookaburra laugh down a bit till I finish my reading?'

Crocodile Dundee looked straight ahead, gave another giggle and went silent. Meanwhile, O'Loan sat with his head bent and his eyes closed, pretending to have dozed off.

The bus continued along its route, stopping now and then to drop off and collect passengers, one of which was a short, stout, balding man in his fifties by the name of Fred Patch. He had loaded a large brown suitcase into the luggage compartment before boarding and making his way up the aisle to sit beside the film addict, who had her head stuck in the newspaper. She shrugged in annoyance as his bulky form pressed heavily against her and snuggled into his seat.

When Fred Patch felt comfortable, he bade her the time of day. 'How are you, wee lassie?' he said in his strong Glasgow accent.

She didn't answer him directly, preferring to clack her chewing gum and mutter to herself, 'Who does Rob Roy think he's talking to? Lassie, the collie dog?'

Fred Patch heard her comment and, smiling, handed her a business card that read *Fred Patch, Buyer and Salesman for the Good Used Clothing Company*. She gave it a quick glance before screwing it up in her hand and dropping it at her feet.

He ignored her and turned his attention across the aisle towards Crocodile Dundee, whose shoulders were shaking with suppressed laughter. Fred Patch leaned across and tapped him on the knee. 'Is there something amusing you, pal?' he asked.

Crocodile Dundee ignored him and went on shaking his shoulders.

Fred Patch looked annoyed and clenched his fists but controlled his fiery temper and resumed his posture. The rest of the passengers just sat absorbed in their own thoughts and devices as the bus sped along towards its destination. Nearing the seaside village of Fahan, many of the passengers were preparing to gather their bits and pieces together, knowing that Buncrana wasn't too far off now.

Fred Patch sat cracking his knuckles and the gum-chewing film addict continued to read. O'Loan was still sitting with his head down pretending to doze.

Crocodile Dundee was now laughing loudly and rummaging about the inside of his shirt with both hands. Frank O'Loan, Fred Patch and the film addict sat upright in unison and stared across at him.

'He has gone stone mad,' said Fred Patch.

Crocodile Dundee was squirming now and screamed with hysterical laughter, 'My pet snake, Willie, he's gone and wrapped himself around me and the cheeky little possum's tickling me to death.'

Suddenly, the bus lurched and screeched to a halt. The driver got out to inspect the wheels. He returned to announce that a tyre had burst and that the passengers should remain in their seats and a replacement bus would take them the rest of the way. Anyone who wished could alight, however, and make their own arrangements to continue their journey.

Fred Patch was the only passenger to leave the bus. He asked the driver to lift the brown suitcase out of the luggage compartment for him but pointed to O'Loan's case, which was the same size and colour as his own.

'Will you continue by taxi, sir?' asked the driver.

'Oh, no. I've arranged to stay here in Fahan overnight at the Red Door Hotel. I have some business to do here.'

O'Loan watched the scene through his window, a contented smile playing across his face. *The suitcase switch is working perfectly,* he thought to himself.

As Fred Patch was walking away with the heavy suitcase, a Garda patrol car pulled up behind the bus and two burly officers emerged and approached it. One of them spoke to the bus driver. 'Having a bit of trouble, then?' he asked.

'I have a flat wheel and have to wait for another bus to transfer my passengers over,' the driver answered, nodding towards the damaged tyre.

The smile faded from the watching O'Loan's face. 'Bloody Guards,' he muttered, sinking into his seat.

Fred Patch looked uneasy, too, and quickened his pace while struggling with the heavy case. He had gone only a few steps when the suitcase handle snapped, the case falling heavily onto the concrete pavement. The impact caused the catches to burst open, allowing the contents to spill out.

Everyone in the nearby bus froze as they watched bundles of banknotes spewing out onto the pavement. O'Loan groaned and sank lower in his seat and the film addict stopped chewing her gum in amazement.

A Guard picked up one of the bundles from the pavement and examined the notes closely. He then looked at Fred Patch, who now stood with his mouth hanging open and still clutching the broken handle.

'To me, these look like part of the twenty-six million pounds haul that was stolen from the Northern Bank not too long ago,' the Guard said. 'I'm afraid we will have to take you to the station to answer a few questions, sir.'

The notes were gathered up and put into two polythene sacks. Fred Patch was handcuffed and placed in the police car which hurriedly whisked him away to the Garda station along with the money.

The watching passengers looked on astounded as the car left the scene with its siren screaming and its blue revolving lights flashing.

A few seconds after Fred Patch was taken away, the crooked bank clerk O'Loan slipped quietly from the bus, unnoticed amid the excited babblings of the passengers, and made a discreet getaway. He went directly towards the Fahan Marina and a waiting yacht that was intended to take Patch on board. O'Loan was soon sailing down Lough Swilly past Dunree Fort and eventually on to a small inlet on the west coast of Scotland where he would disappear for ever.

Fred Patch, the false used-clothes salesman, would later be charged with being a part of an organisation that was assisting in the laundering of the proceeds of the Northern Bank heist.

Meanwhile, as the rest of the passengers waited for the replacement bus to arrive, the young film addict inserted a fresh piece of chewing gum between her teeth. Crocodile Dundee moved in beside her in the seat, still holding Willie his pet snake firmly in his hand. She turned her head towards him and blew a huge bubble that burst about his face. They both went into hysterics, laughing, and instantly fell in love to make a happy ending to my story.

The Intrusion

It was half past midnight when Paul Conway put his key into the lock of his front door. He was tired after walking the two miles from the factory in Pennyburn, where he had clocked out at midnight after another eight hours of the heavy work he had been doing for the past two years since being employed there on shift work.

Paul closed the door silently behind him and entered his small living room after first turning on the light. The smell of toasted bread made by his wife, Rosena, for her and the children's suppers, still lingered in the room. He hung his coat up on the hook behind the door and sat on the sofa to take off his shoes and rest a while with his eyes closed. He felt the tiredness drain from his tense body and savoured the feeling of contentment that allowed the quietness of the sleeping house to bathe his mind, the welcome silence of the room punctuated by the rhythmic ticking of the clock on the mantelpiece.

A few minutes had passed before Paul opened his eyes again, afraid that he would fall asleep where he was sitting. He stood and yawned, stretching his body and limbs as he looked about the room at the faded wallpaper that needed renewed and at the scuffed, worn-out, light-brown-patterned lino on the floor. His eyes roamed around the sparsely furnished living room with its bare Formica-topped, spindly legged table and its four matching, yellow-seated chairs in front of the net-curtained window. It overlooked the small back yard where the coal-house and the shed with its rusted, corrugated tin-roof stood. That was where he stored his toolbox, his children's tricycles and various bits and pieces of wood and toys and tins of paint and brushes.

He squinted up at the off-white, dark-stained ceiling above his head, where a bare, unshaded light bulb hung from a socket at the end of a pair of twisted wires. His gaze lowered again to take in the floor, where, under the table, lay a pair of his eldest son Liam's brown working boots. A tidy row of four pairs of black-polished shoes belonging to three of his younger boys and one little girl lined the front of the fireguard that shielded a still-glowing fire. The shoes were all ready to be worn by them to their schools in the morning. Grey socks and white vests and other light clothes hung neatly from the clothesline strung high across the room. His youngest baby's pram was folded up and leaned against the side of the dark-brown cabinet that stood against the opposite wall facing the fireplace.

Paul felt content and at ease with himself knowing that upstairs in one of the two bedrooms his wife was sleeping soundly while their baby boy slept snug and warm against her. In the front bedroom, two bunk beds and one single bed held the three schoolboys, their bodies untidily sprawled out in various forms while Liam, their 16-year-old brother, would also now be deeply slumbering in another single bed by the front window. In a narrow, rectangular box room above the scullery, Paul's little fair-haired daughter, Aoife, would also be dreaming in her short, cosy bed beside a low sash window.

Paul walked silently in his stocking feet to the scullery and opened the back-yard door and stood outside to look up at the waxing, nearly full moon, whose silvery-blue, even light poured over the back yard, creating dark shadows and even darker corners that concealed the night creatures that lived and crawled along the rough, pitted surface of the back-yard wall. He lit a cigarette and blew a stream of pale-blue smoke into the cool night air, where it drifted slowly upwards towards the watching moon. His cigarette now burnt halfway down, he flicked it from his fingers towards the grating below the scullery window. *Time for bed,* he thought and turned to move inside again. Closing the door softly, he then checked that all was secured before going upstairs to join his sleeping family.

By 5.00 AM all was quiet and peaceful inside the Conway house while outside the night sky had clouded over, leaving only the street lamps to shed their diffused, muted orange light upon the city's now lifeless streets and buildings.

The night's stillness was suddenly disturbed by the whining sound of heavy engines as a convoy of six British Army vehicles made their way from Fort George onto the empty streets. The convoy snaked through the city to take up positions blocking off the street where the Conway home was situated – a cul-de-sac of two rows of terraced houses between Foyle Road and Bishop Street. The two leading vehicles stopped in the middle of the cul-de-sac, where a large number of armed soldiers dismounted to take up station in doorways along each side.

A tall, male RUC officer and a heavy-framed female constable companion alighted from a black armoured car to flank either side of the Conway front door while four soldiers, one of whom is a sergeant, grouped in front of it. The sergeant thumped with a closed fist at the door for ten seconds, a thump for every second, until he stepped aside to make way for a soldier carrying a sledgehammer. He swung it against the door, causing it to jolt violently inwards and slam noisily open against an inner wall. The four soldiers, followed by the RUC personnel, immediately rushed into the house. The sergeant and one of his men ran heavily up the stairs with their guns pointing menacingly forward as the two RUC personnel entered the living room, leaving the two remaining soldiers to take up firing positions towards the stairs.

In the back bedroom, Paul and Rosena, already awakened by the sounds of the front door being forced open, quickly threw on their clothes; their baby and children still slept soundly, unaware of what was happening.

Rosena was first to rush out of the bedroom to be met by the sergeant, who was shouting orders back to his men. She screamed at him: 'What the hell is going on? What are you doing in my home?'

The sergeant shouted back aggressively into her face, 'We have received information that there is a gunman in this house. Now get back into your room.'

Paul, who was now dressed, bounded towards the bedroom door and, seeing the armed soldier behaving aggressively towards Rosena, pulled her back into the bedroom and confronted him, saying, 'There is only one gunman in this house and it's you.'

Immediately, the second soldier, at an order from his sergeant, stepped forward and, using his rifle, robustly pushed Paul and his wife farther back into the bedroom. His sergeant followed them in. By then, Rosena was crying and went to lift her awakened baby, who had also begun crying, from his cot.

The sergeant ordered the soldier to go into the other bedroom where the sleeping boys lay while he escorted Paul, Rosena and the baby downstairs. The four boys in the front bedroom were still sleeping, oblivious to the unnerving, frightening scenes that were being played out when the armed soldier entered shouting, 'Wakey, wakey! Shake a leg! Everybody get up and get downstairs immediately!'

The four boys were slow in stirring, not knowing what was happening in their home. They and Aoife were eventually brought down to the living room, where Aoife ran sobbing to her father and put her arms tightly around his waist. He put a protecting hand on her head, telling her that she was safe with him. Rosena stood protectively clutching her baby boy, who was now crying even louder, and she told Paul that he was hungry.

The RUC woman reached to take the baby from her arms, saying, 'You go ahead and warm him some milk and I'll hold him for you.'

Rosena glared at her in answer, saying, 'You keep your hands off my baby. I can manage without any help from you.' She then proceeded to the scullery to warm some milk. The boys, all in their bare feet and wearing only trousers and light T-shirts, remained silent as they sat on the sofa, yawning and fidgeting with their hair, rubbing their eyes and scratching their legs.

From upstairs, the grumbling sounds of moving

furniture and the heavy boots worn by the soldiers rumbled through the ceiling as they roamed about the bedrooms, emptying drawers and cabinets in their search for literature or any other article that would connect and incriminate any of the Conway family with IRA activity.

An hour and a half had passed when the dawn light eventually began to seep through the slender gaps between the drawn curtains to dispel the dimmer yellow light from the bare light bulb in the room. Soon it would be time for the children's pals to call for them to go to school. Sixteen-year-old Liam, a trainee engineer at one of the government's training centres, was now too late to get his bus.

Meanwhile, the baby had fallen asleep and the boys and Aoife fidgeted and whispered among each other. The two RUC people attempted to make small talk with Paul and Rosena, who both just answered every comment and question with monosyllables and shrugs of the shoulders.

From above the ceiling, the rumbling sounds of the search began to ease slightly and heavy-booted footsteps pounded on the stairs as one of the soldiers came down and into the living room, carrying a grey-painted metal toolbox. He set it on the table before turning and inquiring, 'Who owns this box?'

Everyone looked at one another, but no answer came forth. He asked again in a louder, more commanding voice. 'I asked who owns this box and I need an answer quickly, or else.'

It was then that the youngest boy put his hand up to timidly answer, as if he were at school, 'I own it, it's mine.'

The soldier, now looking angry, asked, 'Well, have you got a key? Hand it over to me.'

Immediately, the boy stood up, took a small key from his pocket and reached it across to the soldier's outstretched hand. The soldier grabbed the key and opened the lock. He looked inside the box and began lifting out and examining its contents, which included small plastic soldiers, a plastic gun, marbles, coins and used postage stamps until finally he lifted out a brown paper bag and opened it slowly.

It contained six eggs.

Holding the bag up, he looked towards the wide-eyed, frightened boy and asked, 'And what are these for? Throwing at policemen or soldiers, eh?'

The boy's eyes filled up as he answered, 'It's my ninth birthday today and I didn't want my brothers to smash eggs on my head for it and that's why I hid them in my box.'

The police officer smiled and lowered his head as the brothers and sister burst out laughing along with their father. Rosena just smiled, being used to such innocent behaviour from her sons. The soldier's face softened with a thin smile on his lips and he put the bag of eggs back into the box, locked it and handed the key back to its now greatly relieved owner.

'You're a wise little fellow,' he said and left the room to go upstairs again.

A few minutes later, loud rapping from the brass knocker on the front door broke the now less tense atmosphere in the room. Paul moved forward to go and answer it but was stopped by the RUC officer, who stepped in front of him.

'Stay where you are,' he said, 'we will attend to it.'

One of the soldiers, who had also heard the knocking, came pounding down the stairs and opened the door a few inches. The half-face and one eye of a small boy peeped in through the narrow opening and a tiny voice asked, 'Are youse ready to go to school yet?'

The soldier, smiling, politely answered, 'Nobody for school today, sonny,' and gently closed the door to return to his duties upstairs.

Meanwhile, outside in the streets, small groups of children were making their way to school and the city was getting noisier and busier as traffic and people now moved to and fro to their destinations.

In the cul-de-sac where the raid was happening, neighbours leaving their homes to go about their daily chores just kept their heads and eyes down as they passed by the military vehicles and alert soldiers. They had seen and experienced it all many times before when the security forces closed off other streets in the area while they searched houses and stopped and searched the residents. The same scenario went on every day and night in many other carefully selected parts of the city.

By half past eight in the morning, the last part of the long operation was nearly at its end when the search of the yard and shed yielded nothing of interest to the soldiers. They moved inside the house again, where all but one were commanded by their sergeant to return and join their comrades in the street.

Paul, feeling relieved on seeing this, looked at Rosena, now more at ease sitting on the sofa nursing her sleeping baby, the boys and their sister gathered around her. None of them seemed fazed with the ongoing ordeal nor had any of them any inkling about the turmoil and mental torture that weighed on their parents' minds and hearts by the invasion and violation of their once happy, peaceful home.

Paul stood in the middle of the floor, waiting for the rest of the intruders to leave his family in peace. But the glimmer of peace and an end to their ordeal were not to last for long as the leading sergeant told their eldest son, Liam, to put on his shoes.

Liam had heard stories of these raids from some of his pals whose families had also gone through the same ordeal more than just once; nightly raids had been a common occurrence in the less well-off communities in Derry ever since the Army had come into the city during the final day of the Battle of the Bogside in 1969. Liam, dressed only in his jeans and a light T-shirt, didn't look at his parents or utter a word but obeyed without question and put on a pair of boots and stood up; he sensed what was about to happen and was ready. The sergeant then announced that Liam was about to be arrested under the Special Powers Act and ordered his remaining soldier to accompany the boy out to the front door. Liam's mother immediately rushed to protect her son but was restrained by the burly RUC woman. Paul also stepped forward to rescue his young son but was stopped in his movements when the tall RUC constable held him in a bear hug.

Liam and the soldier were now gone, the sergeant swiftly following to give out further orders to the rest of his men in the street. Paul and Rosena, who was now sobbing, were released from the grasps of the RUC personnel and told to stay where they were. The RUC pair also followed the soldiers and the boy to the street. Paul didn't wait but followed them to the front door, where the sergeant commanded him not to attempt to come any further. Paul stood just inside his doorway, watching the RUC pair moving off in their black armoured car and then looked towards his son, who was being put into the back of a green Army Saracen.

Liam turned his head and waved a hand to him before the doors were closed and locked behind him. Paul watched, his heart feeling as if it were being torn in pieces, as the heavy, camouflaged vehicle trundled down the street behind the armoured police car to disappear around a corner in a cloud of blue exhaust smoke.

The sergeant, who had all the while been writing on a sheet of paper on a clipboard, approached him and thrust the clipboard into Paul's hand, telling him to sign it. He then handed Paul a counterfoil copy and barked, 'You can also claim off the ministry for expenses incurred for any repairs you get carried out on your front door.' He then ordered Paul to go back into the house, telling him that he should contact the RUC station in Strand Road if he wished to complain about the search and also to inquire about his son. The sergeant wheeled about and ordered the rest of his men to return to barracks. He then boarded a waiting Army vehicle, which moved away to exit the street and area to follow the rest of the convoy back to their base.

Rosena sat sobbing, watched by her young family, as little Aoife put her small arms around her neck. Paul returned from the front door with heaviness in his chest and, leaving the sheet of paper on the cabinet, went to them and encircled them gently with his arms. 'Don't you be crying, now. Everything will be all right again when Liam returns.'

Rosena leaned over and kissed him on the cheek. 'I hope you're right and that God will be on our side. I know that our Liam is a good wee lad and he has done nothing wrong.'

Paul then told the boys to go up and get dressed and that they could stay off school for the rest of the day and that he would make everybody a nice big breakfast.

They scampered up to their bedroom, smiling and excited, to dress and Paul proceeded to the scullery to make breakfast for everyone. After breakfast, Paul and the three boys went upstairs to tidy the bedrooms. Surveying the shambles, the contents of drawers and shelves strewn across the floors and the clothes stripped from the beds, he said, 'No sense in standing looking at it. Let's get stuck in.'

It took an hour and a half to get the rooms straightened out and when they had finished, Paul told the boys that he would give them a bonus along with their pocket money at the end of the week. The boys were delighted and ran down to tell their mother, who was still busy getting the downstairs back into shape. The baby boy lay content in his cot, oblivious to all that had happened.

The rooms at last looking tidier again, Paul began to feel a tiredness creeping over him and sat on the edge of Liam's bed and yawned. His thoughts were whirling inside his head as he went over the unexpected, dramatic events of earlier that morning that had ended with the taking of his eldest son. Looking at his watch, which read 1.30 in the afternoon, he wondered where they had taken him to and hoped that he wasn't being mistreated by his keepers. *I'll go and inquire at the police barracks about his whereabouts and find him and bring him back home again,* he thought. Looking around the rest of the bedroom, he smiled at the array of various photos, souvenirs and artefacts which decorated the walls. Then his eyes fell on the innocent, grey metal toolbox on the floor belonging to his younger boy, peeping out from under one of the bunk beds. It reminded him that today was his son's ninth birthday and he smiled when he thought about the eggs inside it.

He continued looking about the room and smiled at the posters of rock bands and sportsmen that occupied the wall space above Liam's bed. His eyes finally rested on a dark-blue anorak hanging in a corner behind the bed. Leaning across the bed, he lifted the anorak. He gave a loud gasp on seeing underneath, a rifle standing upright against the corner. The sight made every nerve end in his body tighten.

He spoke to himself with tightened jaws: 'How in under heaven's name did they miss this during their search.' He rubbed his eyes, hoping that the gun would disappear and that he had imagined it, but when he looked again, there it was, still standing in the corner, screaming danger at him.

He quickly replaced the anorak over the gun and went downstairs to Rosena working in the scullery. The baby slept in its pram and the boys were out playing in the back yard, Rosena not allowing them into the front street until things had settled back to normality again. He told his wife about his discovery and her knees went weak.

'Maybe the Army has planted it there, Paul. What are we going to do?'

Paul stood facing her. He put his hands on her shoulders and told her to relax and that he would soon find out the truth about how the rifle got into the bedroom. 'In the meantime, I will go to the barracks and inquire about Liam.'

Rosena remained tense and unconsoled.

It was three o'clock in the evening when Paul gained entry to the RUC barracks. There he inquired about his son and was told that he was just about to be released without any charges being made against him. Paul felt relieved and elated when he watched Liam being led out by a stern-faced police man to be handed over to him. He signed a document at the desk and both left for home.

On their way home, Paul asked his son about the rifle and Liam explained why the gun had been hidden there.

'You see, it's not a gun that shoots real bullets, Da. It's a point two-two air rifle that I saved up for over the last year out of my wages. It only shoots wee lead pellets.'

Paul listened intently to Liam, who told him that he had bought the air rifle from a friend in his workplace. His friend was a member of a local air-rifle club and had told Liam that he should join and that he would put his name forward to the committee. A mollified Paul then asked, 'But why did you have to hide it from us?'

'Because I have to get it licensed and was afraid to tell you and my ma in case both of you would make me get rid of it.'

Paul was now more at ease and satisfied with his son's explanation and walked happily back home with his arm around Liam's shoulder. 'Lucky the soldiers didn't find it first or it would have been confiscated and you really would have been in trouble explaining it to them,' he said.

Back at home, Rosena waited anxiously for Paul's return, hoping and praying that he would bring Liam back with him. She heard the front door being pushed open and ran out to greet her now happy, smiling husband and beloved son. The rest of their delighted family gathered round. Peace and happiness returned to the Conway home after going through a dark, frightening ordeal.

The Island Man

Pádraig Ó Catháin lived alone in his small, thatched, whitewashed cottage on Arranmore Island, which faced east across the stretch of moody sea towards Burtonport and the Rosses. Now, at the age of forty-six, he was growing weary of the lonely island life, having lived there with his mother ever since his younger brother, Seán, and his father, Thomas, had perished in their curragh when a storm had visited the island some years before. His mother, Mary Ann, was also now gone to join them, the long years of grieving and harsh life on the island having taken their toll.

He hadn't been across to Burtonport in quite a few years and remembered those many happy days in his youth when his father had taken him and Seán to the fairs every June. On one of those trips, each was given a whole sixpence to buy sweets and lemonade and to throw wooden rings at the hoopla stall in attempts to win one of the glittering bangles or other trinkets to take home to their mother. Once, he did manage to land one of the rings over a little delft cow and remembered the sparkle in his mother's eyes when he proudly presented it to her after they arrived back home that evening. The little cow still took pride of place on the high, turf-smoke-blackened mantelshelf above the open fireplace many long years later.

Now in his mid-forties, Pádraig could see no ease in the poverty and want that pervaded many of the small thatched homes around him. His thoughts were now roaming back over those long, hungry years: rising with Seán and his father before dawn at low tide to carry the seaweed from the shore to the small patch of fertile ground with the lichen-covered, dry-stone wall built around it, that yielded the potatoes and vegetables that sustained them year upon year during the long, harsh winters. He remembered, too, the oh-so-short, warm summers when he would steal away on his own to lay on his back on the sweet-scented heather in the sun and close his eyes and see his childhood friend Julia walking beside him again to school. Or dream about the two of them sailing away in his own boat across the ocean to explore all the exotic countries that he had read about in the school atlas. He would then drift gently back to reality with the sound of his mother's soft voice calling him to return to help his father working in the cow byre.

Pádraig's father also kept poultry and some pigs, their one and only milking cow fending for itself along with their few sheep which grazed on the hillside. They had also willingly shared some of their provisions with their less well-off neighbours. That was the way of people on the island. He remembered, too, climbing down the precarious cliff faces with the other, more daring young men to rob eggs from the screaming gulls' nests; on other days rowing out over the gentle, summer-green sea to lay their baited lines to catch the silvery oil-rich mackerels and hoping to catch the big cod or conger eel that lived in the depths among the wrecks of sunken ships. He often thought, too, about the times when a number of his companions had forfeited their lives in the heart of a sudden storm when the raging sea had swamped their little curraghs as they attempted to make for the safety of the shore. The hardships and tragedies and drudgery seemed to be never ending.

Now in his more mature years, he was alone and grew tired of this kind of life and longed to cross the stretch of deep, uneven water in his curragh to escape from the lonely future on the island. But the past would ever be with him, hanging like an invisible mantle around his broad shoulders to remind him of his status among the peasantry and gentry of the land.

Pádraig now spent too many lonely days sitting outside his cottage door, watching and gazing across the stretch of restless sea at the multi-coloured green hills and purple-blue mountains of County Donegal. He thought many times of Julia, his childhood friend, whom he had grown very fond of when they'd sat beside each other at school. They had remained close friends as they got older, too. Lovely Julia, who kissed him on the lips that morning when she said goodbye to him before stepping onto the curragh that carried her and her older brother Michael to the Burtonport pier from where they would begin their journey to Derry's quay to board the boat to Scotland.

That's where I should be, his thoughts were saying. *I should be happy now along with Julia, wherever she is,* while in his heart the many strands of silver threads that bound each generation to Arranmore held him fast.

It was now early in the spring of the year and Pádraig struggled for a long time between his rebellious mind and his heart's heritage to break the bonds, until at last the longing to leave his home became strong enough. *Leave here and search for Julia, that's what you should have done a long time ago,* his inner self commanded him.

Pádraig's mind was now made up. Within a month he would settle up his affairs on the island and would share out his animals and poultry among his poorer neighbours.

The cottage he would sell to Liam Brady and his four sons; they normally bought up any small pieces of land or property that became vacant. They were the richer inhabitants on the island, being moneylenders as well as hard workers on their land. Liam Brady owned the only shop and public house on the west of the island and it was whispered among the islanders that he was among the elite breed of Donegal's gombeen men.

Pádraig's conscience still nagged at him. He could hear his father's voice calling from among the ghosts of the past: 'You are bound to the island like we were; we all are as the heather and the rocks and the winds a part of it. *Má thréigean tú linn* ... If you desert us our fields will die.'

He felt troubled on hearing his father's scolding and whispered back in answer, 'Is this how they all felt, all those generations of young men and women who had left the island before me? Did they feel the same doubts and hear the same haunting voices of their dead peoples pleading with them to stay?'

Other voices were encouraging and pushing him on, saying, 'To stay for what? Stay and wither away and become a few mere handfuls of earth to be strewn about the hillside with the winter storms? Remember your father and mother and your brother, with only a stone to mark their last place of rest. Where does the dust from theirs and our ancestors' bones lie now? Scattered over the island and drifting in the depths of the living sea.'

His breathing became heavier as he again repeated in a whisper, 'This must have been how those long-gone young men and women before me had all felt before leaving the island. I am no different and I will follow them.'

He then spoke aloud to the silent house. 'I will pretend to myself that I'm crossing to Burtonport to buy some meal for the pigs and hens. Isn't that what island men do to escape from their boredom? Even for a little while? They dream; they pretend. I will do the same. I will go even further than they, and when I get to Burtonport, I will travel on and never return to my island again to live out this useless existence, struggling day by day in poverty and loneliness along with my poor, beloved people.'

***

On a mellow autumn evening, Pádraig Ó Catháin sits alone and at rest outside his cottage door. He listens to the forlorn cry of a curlew overhead as he gazes over the stretch of calm, placid sea that now idles at peace in its low ebb, awaiting the next flow and surge that will renew its unsettledness again. His only companions are his thoughts and he can sense the surge of underlying, unsettling currents within himself beginning to flow again, urging him to leave the island.

'Someday, one of these days,' he whispers to his companions, 'I will leave this lonely island and cross that stretch of green water to Burtonport and move on. Someday soon.'

A soft breeze moves across the heather and brushes alongside his cheek.

Lá éigin go luath (someday soon), it seems to whisper.

The Diamond Tear

Bridget Cole lived in one of those long streets of terraced houses situated between Foyle Road and Bishop Street. She loved the area, especially the friendly people who lived in that part of Derry, and it was so handy to the schools and shops and St Columba's Long Tower Church.

One dull November afternoon, she sat on the low chair by the living-room window, feeding her 5-week-old baby girl, who was wrapped warm and safe in her arms as she softly sang a lullaby. She watched the dark rain clouds drifting slowly across the narrow gap of sky between her own house and the backs of the taller houses in the street behind. The newly built extension to her next-door neighbour's house loomed high to complete one side of the depressing, rectangular skyline.

Bridget and her husband, John, were happily married eight years and had five young children. Their twin boys of one-and-a-half years were sleeping in their blue drop-side cot in a corner of the room. Two other children, both boys, were at school and John was at work in a local builder's yard. It was a tranquil scene, the mother and baby peacefully sitting in the darkening room and yet being bathed in a soft, subdued, fluorescent glow coming through the window from that small patch of sky above the houses.

The baby was sleeping contentedly as Bridget placed her into the crib beside the fire-range. All was quiet except for the ticking of the clock on the wall beside the dresser and the muffled street sounds that drifted in through the windowpanes. It was 1.30 PM and she took out her knitting to finish off another woollen jumper, this one for her eldest child whose seventh birthday fell in a few days' time. The garment finished, she went to the scullery to peel the potatoes over the sink and get everything ready for dinner. As she worked, she looked out of the little window at the drizzling rain falling in a fine spray that covered everything in the yard with a lead-coloured moisture; it even clung to the empty washing line in silvery grey droplets. *What a dismal day,* she thought. *I can't even hang out my washing and the two weans will be coming in from school soaking wet.*

Suddenly, she gave a little shiver and thought, *Someone has just walked over my grave.* It caused a mood of depression to descend on her and she began thinking of all those nice sunny days during the summer when she and John took the children to Fahan where they played all day on the warm, golden sands and splashed in and out of the water. A little tear rolled down her cheek as her eyes filled up but she didn't cry, because she knew from past experience that the present feelings were caused by a mild wave of postnatal depression and wouldn't last long.

She looked at the raindrops gently rolling down the steep dip of the empty washing line and her eye was attracted by one drop that slowly began to glisten. It began to get brighter and brighter until it shone like a polished diamond that emitted a thousand bright rays. One of the rays shone through the small window and reflected off her wedding ring and seemed to light up the whole kitchen. The sun had then thrown a golden beam through a small break in the dark clouds to light up the yard and scullery. Bridget felt a surge of happiness welling up in her breast and throat that made her smile and thank God that she must be the luckiest woman in Derry to have such a good husband and five beautiful, healthy children. The diamond gleamed on the washing line for another few moments before it began to slowly fade away and, a short while later, the sun finally broke through the rest of the diminishing clouds to brighten up the rest of the evening.

The potatoes now peeled, Bridget began to think about the diamond raindrop on the washing line and her thoughts went back through the years until she was a little girl of seven at the Wee Nuns School in the Long Tower Churchyard. Miss McVeigh was reading a poem to the class. It was about a little boy called Hughie being taken on his first day to school by his older brother, his mother waving goodbye to him from the cottage door as he turned the corner past the big turf stack. It was a lovely story and there wasn't a sound to be heard in the classroom from any of the young pupils, so engrossed were they in it. After Miss McVeigh read it, she said that she would be having a little competition in a week's time on the day before the school closed for the Easter holidays. The person who would bring the shiniest object into class that morning would win a framed copy of the poem *Wee Hughie* as well as an Easter egg.

The morning of the competition arrived and the sky was laden with dark, grey clouds and it was drizzling with rain. Most of the boys and girls had brought a shiny object in their school bag. After the morning roll call, which ended with one little boy called Tim O'Kane being marked absent, the usual morning prayers were said before the lessons began. Then Miss McVeigh told the excited children, who were chattering more than usual, to be quiet. The class hushed and Miss McVeigh asked them if they had brought their shiny items with them. After they all answered yes, she made them place their pieces on the big table by the window.

There was an assortment of glass marbles with threads of all beautiful colours inside them, a number of fragments from broken mirrors, paste diamonds and fake pearls from old discarded earrings and necklaces, a small glass slipper that sparkled no matter from where one looked at it, a gold brooch with the diamond missing from it and numerous other beautiful shiny things all arrayed on the table. Miss McVeigh was pleased at the response and smiled as she looked at the sparkling eyes of every child in the classroom.

She stood in front of the big table, looking at each piece and said, 'I'm going to have a very hard time trying to choose a winner from all these beautiful shiny things.'

The pupils went quiet as her eyes slowly moved over each piece, then she asked them to gather round the table and she would pick the piece that belonged to the winner of the competition.

Just then, the classroom door opened slowly and she watched little Tim O'Kane coming in and walk towards them with his head slightly bowed. He stood behind the rest of the children. Miss McVeigh told him to come to the table and asked him if he was all right and why he had come late to school.

'I was searching at home for a shiny thing and couldn't find anything, Miss,' he answered. 'My mother doesn't have any jewels or rings so I had to come on to school without anything.'

Miss McVeigh told him that it was all right, that some of the other children couldn't find any shiny things, either. Then she noticed that he had one hand under his coat.

'What are you hiding under your coat, Tim?'

'It's a little sick bird, Miss. I found it lying on the school steps as I was coming in.'

He took his closed hand from under his coat and opened it to show a little robin redbreast and then he laid it on the table alongside all the other treasures. The other children gathered round closer to look at the robin and the teacher lifted it and examined it carefully. She moved its legs and wings and discovered that it had a broken wing.

'Why, the poor little robin has a broken wing and I'm afraid that it will not live too long,' she said.

Little Tim took it in his hand again and the robin's eyes slowly closed as its head fell to one side. Both he and Miss McVeigh knew that it had just died. The teacher lifted the dead bird from his tiny hand and laid it back on the table. She then looked at Tim and saw a big tear rolling down his cheek. All the children were also looking sad and Miss McVeigh watched the big teardrop slipping from Tim's cheek onto the table. It lay there for a while, just like a silvery grey droplet. Then, slowly, a ray of sunlight that had broken through the dark clouds shone through the window. It fell onto the teardrop and hundreds of brilliant sparkles of coloured crystals shone from it, causing everyone watching to gasp in awe.

A few silent moments passed and Miss McVeigh broke the spell when she put her arm around Tim to announce the winner of the competition to the class.

'I know everybody will agree that the shiniest thing on the table this morning belongs to Tim O'Kane, and he is the winner of the competition.'

The clapping lasted for nearly a minute and slowly faded as Bridget's thoughts returned to the present once more. Her heart was joyful again as she began to hum a little tune while her hands lovingly prepared her family's evening meal.

Jason and Claude

Jason Kyle, a man in his late forties, had been working as a ward orderly in Altnagelvin Hospital for a number of years. Happily married with two children, this was his first day back at work after being off on a week's holiday.

His thoughts were happily recalling the vacation he had spent in Gweedore, in County Donegal, with his wife and children as he and his associate pushed the trolley bearing its unconscious male patient from the operation room to a bed, where they made him as comfortable as could be. Jason wrote the patient's name on a white card, attached it to the wall above the bed and hung the information clipboard on the rail at the foot of the bed. It read: 'Claude Mondell, male, responding normally after having had his appendix removed.' His blood pressure and other health information were also entered on the record sheet.

Jason remained by the patient's bedside, knowing from experience that he would soon be awake and needing attention for a short while until returning to full consciousness. The patient soon began to stir and Jason spoke quietly to him.

'Hello, Mr Mondell, you are doing fine.'

Claude opened his heavy eyelids and groaned.

'Where am I? What time is it? Who are you?'

'You are fine, Mr Mondell,' answered Jason. 'Just relax and breathe slowly. You have had a little operation and will soon be up and about again.'

'An operation?' queried Claude, who was now fully compos mentis. 'I remember now,' he continued, 'I had been walking along Foyle Street and collapsed with a severe pain in my abdomen and lost consciousness.' He tried to rise but Jason gently restrained him.

'I'm afraid you won't be able to sit up for another hour or so, Mr Mondell. But don't worry, you'll be as right as rain soon.'

'But how did you get my name?'

'Your wallet contained all the information we needed. Your name, your address in France and your business cards,' answered Jason.

Claude lay still again and closed his eyes. He was fast asleep within another few minutes and Jason left the ward, content that his patient would be still slumbering when he finished his shift and on his way home to his beloved wife and two adoring children.

***

Next morning at the hospital, Jason did his rounds, seeing to the patients' comforts. He entered Claude's ward and was happy to find him sitting beside his bed on a chair, reading.

'Good morning, Mr Mondell. It's nice to see you up and looking better. Have you had a comfortable night, then?'

'I slept until six this morning and just lay on until I had my breakfast at eight,' replied Claude.

Jason couldn't help noticing that Claude's accent had changed from an Irish brogue the previous evening to a strong French accent now.

'Have you been here in Derry long, Mr Mondell?' he casually enquired.

Claude thought for a few seconds. 'Oh, no, I only arrived two days ago. And what's your name?' he asked.

'My friends call me Jay, but my real name is Jason, so you can just call me Jay, if you wish, Mr Mondell.'

Claude thought for a moment or two before responding. 'Jay. That'll do me fine. I like that name. You know something? I would like to change my name. In fact, I have always wished I were someone else instead of bearing this boring French name, always travelling round the world. Never being able to meet a nice woman to marry and settle down with, own my own chateau, grow grapes and raise children. I think that when I leave here, I will not go back to France ever again. I will become a different person entirely. I will live in Dublin and find a good position there, meet and marry an Irish colleen and become very wealthy and happy.' He paused for a moment. 'Oh, by the way, Jay, I must ask you a very important question: was there any money in my wallet when I was brought here?'

Jason was frowning as he placed his hand against Claude's temple to feel if it was overly warm. 'There was a lot of money and traveller's cheques, Mr Mondell, and they are safely locked away until they're returned to you on leaving the hospital. Nevertheless, I am interested in your health and must take your temperature, I suspect that you mustn't be as well as you think you are.'

He took the thermometer from Claude's mouth and saw the reading was normal.

Jason frowned and thought, *His conversation doesn't seem to be normal, saying that he will change his identity and stay here in Ireland and live in Dublin. Normal people just don't reveal such private feelings to strangers. There's something not right about this Claude Mondell and I must report his condition to my superiors at once.*

An hour after Jason reported Claude Mondell's odd behaviour, two policemen entered the ward. One of them smiled as he saw Claude sitting by the bed.

'Well, then, *Mr Mondell* … or should I say, Mickey "The Squirrel" McBride? We have finally caught up with you and, better still, the Frenchman's wallet that he reported missing to us yesterday has turned up in your possession as well. How coincidental! Now that we have found you and the wallet, one of our men will be waiting here in the hospital until you are fit and well enough to go to court and then hopefully spend a few months convalescing in Crumlin Road Prison.'

It turned out that Claude Mondell, alias Mickey McBride, was one of the most notorious pickpockets in Derry.

McBride was speechless as he sat with his mouth wide open.

Meanwhile, Jason, who was pretending to tend to another patient in another bed, was listening to every word. He smiled as he eventually arrived at McBride's bedside.

'How are you feeling now, *Mr Mondell*?'

The Squirrel gave him a painful look before replying sourly, 'I'm feeling very sick indeed, and utterly deflated into the bargain.'

Jason, whose shift was now over, was on his way out of the ward, but before leaving, he stopped and turned round to bid Mickey a farewell in a French accent.

'So you are leaving us, Meester Squeerrel. I hope you will enjoy the rest of your stay in one of our finest Ireesh hotels. *Bon voyage.*'

To which McBride responded by giving him a very unfriendly two-finger gesture.

Eddie's Bad Fortune

Eddie had won five million pounds on the Lotto exactly ten years ago to the day. And what excitement and commotion it had stirred among Eddie's family and friends and in the local media. He was even interviewed on Channel 9 Television and was given valuable advice on how to manage his unexpected fortune.

The publicity struck him like a whirlwind, turning his life upside down. Eddie paid off all debts for his parents, his brothers and sisters, threw parties for his relations and pals, donated cheques to charities, travelled all over Ireland and far beyond, until three years had whizzed by and his feet finally came to rest again on his own dear Derry soil.

'Wow! What an exciting experience it is, being thrust from rags to riches overnight!' he kept repeating to himself.

And now it was time to take stock of his life before he lost contact with all of his real friends and ended up dead in another couple of years if he didn't slow down. That is when he met his Mary of the 'curling fair hair and sparkling eyes' who worked in the Star shirt factory on the Foyle Road.

She caught Eddie's eye one wet evening when he was sitting in his car in John Street after a meeting with his bank manager. The rain was bouncing off the ground and she was sheltering in a shop doorway, her wet hair framing an angelic, heart-shaped face, showing no signs of make-up.

He had a strong urge to meet her; some unknown, uncontrollable force took over and he just had to talk to her. He rolled the car window down; Mary was looking at him as he beckoned her to come in out of the rain. Innocently, she came and sat beside him, her presence filling the car with her pleasant, damp fragrance. That was his first encounter with the gentle, modest lady, who knew Eddie by name, having seen his picture in the newspapers after he had won the Lotto.

Leaving her to the door of her home, he arranged to meet her soon. Mary avoided his advances at first, knowing that he was a rich man and had acquired a reputation for being a high flier and having an eye for the gentler sex.

Eddie eventually convinced her that he had settled down and they became close friends. A few beautiful months followed, during which he took her out to dinner and offered her some modest presents, having enough sense not to over-lavish her, knowing that she came from the same humble background as he did.

He was now a regular visitor to her family home, where he became a part of the household. Both her parents and her two brothers and younger sister treated him with great respect. Likewise, his own family accepted Mary so much that he gained enough confidence to ask her to marry him.

Fulfilling Mary's wishes, the wedding was a modest affair and they moved into a terraced house in the Bogside. Eddie eventually became his old self again, picked up on his old lifestyle and was the happiest rich man in Ireland. Money couldn't buy what he had, and he was content that his wealth had played no part in winning Mary: it was Eddie and not his riches she married. He had modest ambitions, content to take one or two foreign holidays a year. His only true wish was that he could have a son. Alas, that was not to be.

Four years passed and it gradually began to gnaw at his heart until his mind was in turmoil. He began to question Mary, as if she were to blame for their childless marriage. One day he said to her, 'We have more money that anyone could ask for, but still you cannot bear a single child like any other woman.'

Mary just kept her silence and bowed her head.

Eddie became obsessed about not having any offspring and their marriage started to fall apart. After another year, he began to party and run around again with his old friends in a bid to regain his old, happy, carefree self. He was on a slippery slope to nowhere. He thought, *Where is the happiness all this money was supposed to bring?* His family became estranged to him as he became more selfish in his alcohol-soaked mind and rejected the only true friends that he had ever had in his life. Little did Eddie realise at that stage that he was very ill. Eventually he had to go into a rehabilitation centre.

Mary was still in love with him; she told him so every time she visited him. But Eddie kept hurting and rejecting her until, as the days went by, he did not recognise her as his wife. On each visit she deteriorated in spirit and physical appearance. She was losing weight, her voice was weakening and the sparkle no longer brightened her eyes.

It was shortly after he was admitted to a mental institution that Mary's visits ceased. His Mary of the curling hair had lost hope in Eddie and of ever having a child and remained heartbroken and lonely until she lost all interest in herself and became a recluse.

Eddie had been rich for a little while and now the only real treasure that he had ever possessed he had lost.

Eddie still had vague memories of the excitement that lifted his being all those years ago when he had wished for the magic Lotto numbers that would make him the happiest man in Ireland. Vague, fleeting glimpses now and again crept into his recollections of a fair-haired angel that once filled his days and nights with love and happiness.

Did I really have five million pounds, or is that some lingering figment of my imagination in my tired mind? was a question he asked himself daily. *Where have those years gone?* he would also ask as he awakened to another day, to the same old routine that kept him busy and sane. Rising at six o'clock in the mornings to shower, shave, dress, have breakfast while listening to the distant, low sounds of music from a speaker on the ceiling and wait as he rocked to and fro, to and fro in his chair in his little room.

Just what am I waiting for? I have forgotten. I am thirsty and tired. Oh, what I wouldn't give for just one more sip of wine …

Florrie's Number

Florrie Cullen, an elderly spinster lady of seventy-plus, had been emptying the stale water from the porcelain flower vase when it slipped from between her long, weak, bony fingers. 'They say everything happens in threes,' she muttered to herself as she lifted the dead chrysanthemums and set them onto the draining board. 'What have I done to deserve this? Someone must have put the evil eye on me,' she cursed under her breath. 'Well, bad cess to them, whoever they are.'

She picked up the broken pieces from the sink and placed them on a piece of cardboard, which she carried along with the dead flowers outside to the rubbish bin. As Florrie approached the back door again to enter her kitchen, it slammed shut, causing its pane of glass to fall out and shatter at her feet on the hard concrete. 'Holy God Almighty,' she cried. 'Bad luck is with me today all right.'

She proceeded to brush up the debris and put it into her bin. 'Please let that be the end of it,' she prayed as she returned indoors, where she took her rosary beads from their little brown leather purse on the kitchen table. *I'll say a decade or two and maybe my luck will change,* she thought and sat down on her favourite wooden chair.

Florrie had just begun the first Hail Mary when one of the chair legs broke, sending her tumbling to the floor. There she lay for a few minutes until the shock subsided and she knew that none of her bones were broken. Poor Florrie struggled to her feet again. 'I'm all right,' she said, smiling to herself and feeling her ribs and shoulder with her thin, pointed fingertips. 'The wee prayer must have done me good. Three pieces of bad luck have visited me today and tomorrow it will be some other poor unfortunate person's turn. I got off lightly when I think about it, because my big number hasn't come up yet.'

A moment or two later, while Florrie was putting on the kettle for a cup of tea, she fell again. Instantly, she heard a voice from above booming out.

'Who said bad luck always only comes in threes? I will decide on that – and on whose last number will be drawn. And when. And as for you, my good servant Florrie Cullen, you will know yours is up when you hear the Grim Reaper knocking on your heart.'

Poor old Florrie pulled herself up from the floor, sat on her chair, blessed herself and said, 'Thank you, Lord. Now I will enjoy my wee cup of tea.'

No sooner had Florrie finished her last words when she heard the knocking on her heart and in her ears. The Grim Reaper had come to claim another soul.

Florrie's number had finally arrived!

The Glamour Boy

I met Joe Mackey briefly about six months ago for the first time in four years and, to tell you the truth, he looked every bit the happy-go-lucky man I used to know in his heyday. He was sitting in Tesco's foyer with three or four bags of groceries at his feet and I would have walked past him if he hadn't called my name.

'Jeez, Joe,' I said, 'is this what you're at now, sitting looking round you in supermarkets and guarding bags of shopping for the wife?'

He laughed heartily – to cover his embarrassment, I presumed – because Joe, in his earlier years, was regarded as a man's man. 'No ould shopping or sissy stuff for me,' he used to preach. 'That carry-on is only for henpecked men and wimps.' That was his attitude to life. 'Leave the shopping and housework for the women to do, and we men will attend to the important affairs of running the country and going to war,' was what he had always expounded.

Those serious worldly matters were thoroughly discussed daily in the bookies and in the Central Bar three or four nights a week by Joe and his drinking friends before returning half-cut to their homes and laying down the law, just to let the women know that men still ruled the roost. He and his drinking pals were up to all the scams of the day, every one of them doing the double and living rent-free; and all of them smoked like chimneys. Joe took three continental holidays a year and, when he wasn't away, both he and she would stay in their mobile home in the Downings, where he had another circle of similarly inclined friends. Mind you, he always made sure that his mother-in-law lovingly looked after their three children, who were still at school.

Joe always dressed well, his hair neatly groomed, and any stranger looking at him would have taken him for a very successful businessman or some important professional. All in all, Joe was right and heavy on the drink and I wondered why his inner self didn't seem to notice or rebel against his abuse of it. He looked so amazing for his age that you would have thought that he had been blessed with some special gene to control his immune system.

In a way, I sort of envied Joe when I looked at my own situation. Here I was with nine weans and labouring as a navvy six days a week on a building site and coming home in the evenings, knackered. If anyone had asked me to go out for a drink during the week, I would have had to refuse: firstly because of lack of sufficient pocket money, and secondly because I would have been too tired the next day and wouldn't have been able to function properly and might have been given the sack. I was always very conscious of that, my first duty being to my wife and family.

Looking at Joe and my own reflection in a shop window that day, the comparisons between us were extremely different. There was Joe, a year or two my senior, looking like a glamour boy and here was me feeling and looking like a worn-out and shabbily dressed pauper. I had two more years of hard slogging to endure before my retirement, and was hoping I could last till then.

I saw Joe again yesterday. His dark-tinted, wavy hair was perfectly shaped and his peach-coloured skin glowed with not a wrinkle to betray his sixty-five years. He wore a well-fitted, light-tan cashmere suit, a pale-brown tie and a pale-cream-coloured shirt. A stranger would have guessed his age to be about forty-one, he looked so well. There he was, the picture of health, which was amazing, considering his lifestyle, and now he looked so at peace with himself and the world as he lay in his beautiful, walnut-coloured coffin, waiting to be taken to the graveyard and to face his maker.

I didn't envy him as much at that moment as I said a wee prayer over him. 'There but for the grace of God go I,' I prayed, placing a Mass card at his feet.

Then, turning away from him, the oft-repeated, wise old saying crossed my mind: you can't judge a book by its cover.

Dublin Break Away

Julia Robbins shuffled across her little kitchen in her old, battered house slippers. She hummed a little tune to herself as she laid the table for her husband, Sammy, who would just now be getting dressed in the bedroom before stomping down the stairs for his breakfast.

They were together now forty-nine years and their family of two boys and a girl were all married and living in the town. Julia, now nearing her seventy-fourth year, was beginning to feel her age, although she was very happy and content living in her small terraced house in Rosemount with Sammy, still right and sprightly, despite his being a few years her senior. He was a kind and gentle man who greeted her every morning with, 'Well, Julia, how are you this morning?' And, before she could answer, he would add, 'Glad to hear that. Isn't it another nice morning to be alive and well?'

Then one morning out of the blue, she quickly answered, 'Aye, it is great to be alive and well, all right, but do you know something, Sammy? Do you not think it's about time we would need to be taking a wee trip away somewhere, just for a change, you know, even for one day?'

Sammy set his cup on its saucer and let her words sink

in for a moment or two before answering. 'Begad, Julia, I think you're right. I was just thinking about that meself the other day. I thought to meself it must be nearly a year ago since me and you went on that bus to Buncrana for the day last April.'

Julia sat down opposite him at the table and took a sip from her cup; she knew he was just as anxious as her to get away from the house as well, even for one day.

'It's not that I don't love my wee house,' she said with a tinge of guilt while looking around her spotlessly clean kitchen, 'but sometimes I feel that we should go out now and then to see how the world is getting on out there. And as for you, Sammy, the only distance you go is down to the bottom of the street in the mornings to get your newspaper and to watch the traffic going past.'

Sammy agreed with her and slapped his knee with the palm of his hand, saying, 'You are right, Julia. And do you know what? We'll use our bus passes and take a trip to Dublin tomorrow morning. And do you know what else we'll do, Julia? We'll stay for a night in the Gresham Hotel in O'Connell Street. Now, what do think of that?'

Julia was smiling broadly by now and her eyes twinkled with delight as she responded, 'Oh, Sammy, that's a lovely suggestion. And we can go to the Dublin Zoo and see the giraffes and elephants and seals and feed peanuts to our monkey relatives.'

Sammy laughed and began adding his own plans.

'We can also go to Stephen's Green and sit by the pond and watch the people go by and the ducks being fed. Then, if we feel a bit peckish, we'll go and have a snack in the Stephen's Green Centre.' He paused for a second to think of some other places they could visit before continuing. 'One other place I would love to visit,

Julia, is the National Museum, to look at the ancient artefacts and paintings and the famous Bog Man.' Julia listened intently as he paused for another moment or two before going on. 'I would especially like to see the Ardagh Chalice and the gold hoard that some farmer ploughed up in one of his fields some fifty years ago.'

Julia couldn't contain her excitement and quickly rose from her chair to clear the table. 'Oh, Sammy, it'll be wonderful. I can't wait till tomorrow morning.'

She continued to talk as she carried her cup and saucer to the kitchen sink. Then, without warning, the two pieces of delft fell from her hands and smashed into smithereens on the tiled floor. Sammy rose quickly and went to her assistance. Taking her gently by the elbow, he led her to her soft chair by the window.

'It's that old arthritis in my hands starting to play up again, Sammy,' she said with a tinge of sadness.

Sammy eased her down onto her chair and consoled her, saying, 'Don't you be worrying yourself about that, Julia. Sure we have dozens more cups and saucers in the china cabinet and we never even use them.'

Julia rubbed the back of her hands as Sammy swept up the broken pieces. When he had finished and cleared the rest of the table, he took her hands in his and looked at them. 'The joints aren't as swollen as they were six months ago, Julia. Maybe it was just the excitement of tomorrow's trip that made you drop them,' he said, attempting to cheer her up.

'Maybe so, Sammy,' Julia agreed, 'because I don't feel that old nagging arthritic pain in them that I used to have before I began taking the tablets.'

***

The next morning, Julia and Sammy alighted from the bus outside the Gresham Hotel and made their way to the reception desk, where they checked in and received the key to their room. They unpacked, made a cup of tea and sat down to relax for a while before changing into casual clothes and going for a stroll along the bustling O'Connell Street towards O'Connell Bridge. They crossed the bridge and soon were in Grafton Street, enjoying the buskers and the fashion displays in the windows of the expensive shops. They gradually moved towards St Stephen's Green, where they sat on a summer seat by the pond and spent almost an hour watching people passing by and the ducks being fed. Sammy held Julia's hand.

'Isn't this what we've been longing for, Julia, when we sat in our wee kitchen? And now here we are together, fulfilling our dream.'

In answer, Julia laid her head on his shoulder and gently pressed his big, soft hand. 'It's like heaven, Sammy. And to think we'll have the whole of tomorrow as well to see all the things we've been longing to see.'

After breakfast the next morning, they went to the zoo in Phoenix Park, where they spent nearly two hours looking at the giraffes, elephants, seals and birds, and where Julia fed peanuts to their monkey relations. They then boarded a bus to the National Museum, where they looked at the Ardagh Chalice and the ancient Bog Man that lay prostrate in a glass case. They browsed for nearly an hour until Julia began to feel a bit tired and needed a wee cup of tea and a bun.

As they made their way to the museum café, Julia spotted a blue-patterned vase on a white marble stand. It was on display in the middle of a small alcove behind a rope cordon. 'Oh, Sammy,' she said, 'would you look at that beautiful vase in there? Wouldn't it just look lovely sitting in the middle of our wee kitchen table with a nice bunch of chrysanthemums in it? I wonder if it's for sale.'

They went closer to get a better look. Sammy read the small sign in front of the vase. 'It says it's from the Ming Dynasty, wherever that is.'

Julia stepped over the low rope cordon to get a closer look and lifted the vase from its marble pedestal. 'Oh, Sammy, you know it's just the kind of vase I've been wanting for years,' she said, holding it out in front of her to view at arm's length.

Sammy hesitated. 'It is lovely, all right, but I don't think it would be for sale, not in here in the museum.'

Just then, his eyes opened wide in horror as he watched the vase fall as if in slow motion from Julia's hands to land at her feet, where it smashed into a thousand pieces around her. Two attendants, hearing the noise and commotion, immediately confronted them and led Julia and Sammy by the arms to a small office. Sammy and Julia were frightened, not knowing what to do or say. One of the attendants questioned them, asking their names and address and why they were in Dublin. Sammy answered all his questions. The attendant then asked Julia about her reasons for lifting the vase.

'Did you not realise that Ming vase was made over five hundred years ago?' he added

Julia paused a while to let his words sink in and gave a great sigh of relief before answering.

'Thank goodness to hear you saying that, sir, for you've just put my mind at ease. I was very worried, thinking that it was a new vase.'

The four looked at each other in silence for a few moments before Sammy and the two attendants broke into fits of laughter at her innocence. One of the attendants, with a wink to Sammy, then said, 'Lucky for your missus the vase is well insured or you would have been paying up for it for the rest of your days.'

Needless to say, they were allowed to have their tea and buns in the museum café before being led gently to the front entrance and advised to stay away from the National Museum for a long time.

***

Back in their home in Rosemount again a couple of days later, Sammy couldn't take the smile off his face as he looked at the replica Ming vase he had bought in a second-hand shop before leaving Dublin. It was sitting on a pretty emerald-green doily in the middle of the table, proudly displaying a lovely bunch of fresh chrysanthemums. Julia sat opposite him, contently rubbing some cream on her arthritic finger joints.

'Sure that's a far nicer looking vase than that old cracked relic that was sitting in the Dublin museum just waiting for someone like me to put it out of its miserable existence,' Julia laughed.

Sammy nodded in agreement and smiled, a little twinkle in his eye.

The Paper Boat

When Barry Carlin's mother Ann died, it didn't worry him. He was just five at the time and a child of that age held no notions or fears about death.

Of course, he knew that something was wrong. Visitors came at all times of the day to the house and got cups of tea and small sandwiches and pastry. They looked at Barry and whispered to each other as if he had done something bad. He wondered why. Was it some kind of holy day or near Christmas again? He knew it wasn't Easter because he would have been given some chocolate eggs. Maybe it was St Columba's Day? But then it couldn't be because everyone would be wearing an oak leaf in their buttonhole or pinned on their cap. And his street would be decorated with green and yellow and blue bunting. There would be a parade to the chapel, and men would carry banners with St Columba's picture and God Bless Our Patron Saint of Doire printed on them. He wished that it was, so that he could walk behind a banner with his father, Tom, and listen to the accordion band playing sweet music, the kind of music that always made him feel happy.

But somehow it didn't seem like a holy day: people were always happy then instead of having frowns on their faces and whispering to each other going up and coming down the stairs. Some even had tears in their eyes. No, it couldn't be a holiday.

It was then his younger sister, Jane, came running into the house from the front street where she was playing. She was crying and screaming for her ma. Barry took her hand to lead her up the stairs to see her. He also wanted to see if his ma was in bed sick again. They were halfway up the stairs when Uncle Dan stopped them, saying, 'Where are yeese goin, wee son?'

'We're goin up to see my ma,' answered Barry. 'Our Jane wants her and I want to talk to her and give her a hug to make her throat better.'

'You can't see or talk to her the night,' said Uncle Dan.

'Not even the night, even when our wee Jane is crying for her and needs her?'

'Not even the night or any other night or even the morrow.'

'But why?'

'Because she's away up to heaven and she's watching over you and your little sister Jane and your da. She's looking down now and every day from up there.' Uncle Dan said it quietly as if he were praying.

'But I didn't even see her going,' complained Barry and turned to tell Jane who, like Barry, didn't understand.

Next day, when Barry's wee school friends came to the house, they filed past his mother's coffin with frightened faces. Barry was allowed to join them. He just stood and looked at her long, dark eyelashes and closed, unblinking eyes. He looked at her unmoving, deep-pink lips that played him tunes every morning and wondered why his uncle had told him and little Jane that his ma was up in heaven.

It was the first time in Barry's life that he had strange feelings inside him and they kept him from speaking or crying. And when his da and his uncle and other men carried out the big brown box with the golden handles and cross on it, Barry knew that his ma was inside it, and knew, too, that he would never see her ever again. She was only twenty-five then. And they were taking her to heaven.

There were lots of very special memories Barry had of his ma, little cameos that he kept in a special album in his heart. His eyes would glaze as he remembered them when he was playing or sitting on his da's chair. His ma showing his little sister Jane how to put on her shoe or showing him how to scribble with one of his crayons on a page from one of his da's discarded newspapers. Every morning after breakfast, his mother would sit on the sofa and play an old Irish air on her penny whistle. In the middle of a tune, she would sometimes take the whistle from her smooth, red lips and sing words to the rest of the tune.

> *'The minstrel boy to the war has gone,*
> *In the ranks of death you will find him.*
> *His father's sword he has girded on,*
> *And his wild harp strung behind him.*
> *Land of song cried the warrior bard,*
> *Though all the world betrays thee.*
> *One sword at least my right shall guard,*
> *One faithful harp shall praise thee.'*

'Playing her whistle when she should be out brushing the front of her house or looking after her weans,' their next-door neighbour Mrs O'Reilly would be overheard sneering to one of the other neighbours. But Ann Carlin knew that it was good to begin the day with a tune or a song and her gait was always sure and straighter than others in the street.

Barry's da worked on one of the cargo boats that plied between the ports of Derry and Glasgow. Often on his journeys, Tom would pass his spare time whittling pieces of wood, turning the pieces into little animals, birds and dolphins. Then when he came home at the weekends, he would hide some in various places about the house so that Barry would come across them. Often when he opened his box of crayons or put his tiny hand into a drawer or into the biscuit barrel, Barry would find a little wooden creature. His blue eyes would blink in surprise and ask his mother where it came from. She would always answer with the same white lie: 'The fairies must have put it there for you, Barry.'

Then there were times when he learned his prayers from his mother every morning while he sat on the edge of the table, wearing his pyjamas as she stood protectively in front of him, combing his soft fair hair. He listened and looked innocently into her gentle blue eyes and repeated every line. He still remembered them.

> *'Oh, Angel of God, my guardian dear,*
> *To whom God's love commits me here.*
> *Ever this day be at my side,*
> *To light and guard,*
> *To rule and guide.*
> *Amen.'*

Today's parents may smile and say that it would be too old fashioned to teach their children such prayers in the morning and at bedtime, but, in fact, that's how all children learned their prayers for hundreds of years.

In the days after their ma had gone, Jane was watched by Aunt Mary, who lived at the top of the street, while Barry was at school. His da had to leave the house early each morning to board the boat that left at 8.00 AM on the dot for Glasgow. It was seven in the evening when his da returned to take charge of them again. There was an awful longing and loneliness in Barry's young heart in those empty days which made him feel as though it would break in two.

It was not long after that Aunt Mary told him that his da had to leave on a bigger boat, a liner, to go on a long sea journey. His da took him down to the Derry quay to see the big ship a week before it sailed. It didn't look like a boat at all. It looked like a big row of houses with three big chimneys between them and he wondered how such a huge, heavy-looking iron monster could float across the deep, green ocean.

The next week, his aunt and da took him and little Jane down to the docks. His da hugged them and pressed a half-crown into Barry's hand. They watched as the massive ship moved slowly down the River Foyle and he saw his da waving to them from the stern. Everyone on the quay was waving and cheering and a band was playing. They all seemed to be so happy and he wondered why.

A week after his da had sailed away, Aunt Mary took wee Jane and him up to Brooke Park, where they looked through the netting wire into the fishpond to see the golden fish swimming below the green lily pads. 'Are there any green lily leaves on the sea where my da is crossing?' His aunt just looked and smiled at his innocence and patted his fair head.

When they went back home, she made him a paper boat to sail in the bath and left him there to play with it.

Barry leaned over the edge, set his boat into the water and it floated. He pushed it along with a pot stick until it bumped into the other end of the bath. Soon, the paper got too wet and the boat began to sag until it listed to one side and sank. It was then that Aunt Mary came into the bathroom with a deep frown on her face to see the boat sinking.

'So your paper boat has sunk, wee man.'

Barry just looked up at her and nodded. His eyes glistened as tears filled them. Mary bent down and put her arms around him. 'Never mind, Barry. That's what some boats do, even big ones.' There was sadness in her eyes and her voice was shaking. 'Remember the big ship that your da went down the river on last week?'

He nodded and looked at his sunken boat, now a sodden jotter page again.

'Well, that big boat has sunk as well. It … it sank, just the same as yours.'

Barry hesitated as he thought about it for a few seconds. 'Then, that means my da will have to come home again, won't he?'

'No … no, Barry. He was drowned,' she sobbed.

Barry looked at her, puzzled. 'Did his suitcase and box of tools drown, too?'

'Yes, Barry, everything sank with the boat.'

Barry felt very annoyed about his da's toolbox and suitcase being sunk. He was annoyed about his da as well.

'Come on downstairs and I'll make you a better boat,' Mary said.

'No, Auntie Mary. I don't like boats anymore.'

He began crying loudly and tears rolled down his cheeks.

'I hate boats and don't want to ever see one again.'

Before he went to bed that evening, Barry lifted his

pillow, as he always did, to see if any spiders were hiding beneath it. His eyes opened wide in surprise. Underneath were two little wooden ducks and a wooden dolphin – all had been whittled by his father's hand.

Barry smiled as he laid his head on his soft pillow. He dreamed that he walked with little Jane along the quay and two small ducks followed behind. They stopped when he heard his da calling from a huge, white, paper boat that floated up the river and docked beside them. His da waved to them and soon they were beside him on the boat, which began to sail on up the river with the two ducks swimming beside them. In front of the boat, a dolphin surfaced to lead them as they went.

'Where are we going to, Da?' he asked.

'Up to the very top of the River Foyle, where heaven is, son, to see your ma.'

'And will she be playing her penny whistle, Da?'

'She will be, son, and she will be singing as well.'

Soon, the dolphin stopped swimming; the boat stopped sailing, too, and Barry could hear music being played on a penny whistle.

He looked towards the shore and his ma was waving to them and she began to sing. Barry was very happy and looked to where his da had been standing beside him.

He was gone.

When Barry looked to the shore again, his da was waving to him from beside his ma. Barry called to them to come and join him and wee Jane, but the boat became waterlogged and began to sink. He didn't feel afraid: he knew that his da and ma were near.

Barry woke for a few seconds from his dream, feeling happy, and in his hand he clasped a little wooden dolphin. He yawned, content, knowing that both his da and his ma were watching and smiling down on him and little Jane, and soon fell fast asleep again.

Murder in the Algarve

Lewis Parker and his wife, Sue, were on their first holiday together since their marriage two years previously. They had been here once before, a week in the Algarve on their honeymoon, and were familiar with the hotel and the locality. It was really a second honeymoon that Sue had suggested they have, although she didn't fully reveal to him her true reasons for wanting to go.

It was their second evening and they were having a quiet drink in the hotel bar, making plans about some interesting places to go the next day, when Lewis spotted a young lady he had met the first time they were there. Teresa Du Maurier was her name and they had befriended her and her mother. They were French and lived in the Algarve and, although they had all promised to keep in touch, they never did. She was sitting alone at a table not too far away. Lewis drew Sue's attention to her and nodded in return as the lady gave him a weak smile. Sue showed no emotion nor did she indicate any recognition of the French woman. It was as if she were deliberately ignoring the other lady's presence or genuinely didn't remember Teresa Du Maurier.

Lewis dabbed his mouth with a tissue. 'I must go over and say hello,' he said airily, rising from his chair.

Sue had fire in her eyes as she caught his hand and reprimanded him through clenched teeth. 'Don't you dare leave me sitting here alone while you approach that woman, panting like a little schoolboy.'

Lewis sat down again, a look of surprise on his face.

'What's the matter with you, Sue? I didn't mean to upset you. Please forgive me if I did, but I just wanted to say hello from us both.'

Sue relented. 'I'm sorry for snapping at you, Lewis. Let's forget about it and enjoy the rest of the evening. We can say hello to her another time.'

It was much later, and they had had taken a few more drinks than their usual quota, when Sue went to the powder room. She happened to see Teresa Du Maurier standing in front of the mirror touching up her lipstick. The woman eyed Sue's reflection and, without turning around, spoke into the mirror.

'Hello, Sue. Remember me?' she asked in a purring French accent.

Sue stopped and looked at the lady smiling at her from the mirror.

'Why? Should I remember you?' she replied with a touch of sarcasm.

The French lady turned to face her and Sue saw that she was a very beautiful young woman. The same beautiful woman who was the very reason Sue came back to the Algarve again.

'I do remember you, now that I think about it. And how is your mother? Keeping well, I hope?' The last sentiment was a lie, because Sue didn't give a damn for this woman or her mother.

Du Maurier answered her with a tinge of sadness. 'My

mother passed from this world not too long ago, just three years after dear Papa's demise. I'm all alone now and spend most of my spare time visiting hotels. You see, I love meeting people, especially Irish people like you and Lewis.'

Sue offered her condolences, feeling guilty about thinking so negatively about the lady's mother. After all, she reasoned, the older woman had been very courteous to Sue and Lewis that last time they'd met. She couldn't say the same about the beautiful woman who now stood so close to her in the hotel powder room. This woman who had haunted her dreams so many times in the past two years. This woman whose existence had obsessed Sue's mind so much that she was driven to persuade Lewis to return to this very hotel, pretending to him that it was to be their second, romantic honeymoon.

Sue returned to join Lewis, who waited lovingly for her at the small table in the lounge bar. He wasn't aware that Sue had met Teresa Du Maurier in the powder room and that Teresa had also returned to the lounge. The evening progressed pleasantly enough between them and they talked and remembered little pleasantries and romantic moments from their last visit to the Algarve.

It was now nearing midnight and they were longing to return to their bedroom when Teresa Du Maurier came to interrupt their romantic mood. She didn't look too steady as she came to their table and asked if she could join them. Lewis knew that she was drunk and helped her to sit in one of the low lounge seats.

'Hello, darling,' she slurred in her soft, sexy French accent. 'I'm so glad you have come back to see me again.'

Sue was furious but held her tongue. She remembered the last encounter she had with Du Maurier when she was with Lewis on their honeymoon. She remembered how this woman had lured Lewis to her bedroom on the false pretence that a cat had been under her bed. Lewis had fallen for her ruse and ended up locked in the room along with her.

Now was Sue's moment to get her revenge. 'I'm afraid you need to go to your room,' she advised.

Du Maurier answered, 'I won't be going to my room alone. I want Lewis to take me there and I can assure you that I will return him to you in one piece.' She was smiling broadly now, which made Sue very angry.

'*I'll* leave you to your room,' Sue hissed sharply. 'Lewis is not that kind of man. And anyway, I want to speak to you about a certain matter.'

Lewis helped Teresa to her feet and both he and Sue walked her to the lift. He helped her into it and stepped out, leaving Sue to take Teresa to her room.

***

Next morning, the guests were alerted by the screaming of an ambulance siren at the front of the hotel. It wasn't until it had left, bearing a body covered with a blanket on a stretcher, that they discovered from the staff in the breakfast restaurant that a woman had been found dead in her bathroom by one of the cleaning ladies. She was hanging from the showerhead by a length of curtain cord around her neck. The woman was a regular visitor and was known to have had a slight mental illness that began after the death of her mother. Foul play was not suspected.

Sue smiled on hearing the news, but Lewis was numb. 'She was perfectly compos mentis, although a bit tipsy, when you left her to her room last night,' he said in disbelief.

Sue agreed. 'She seemed quite all right to me when I left her at her door. Why, she even thanked me and bade me goodnight.'

Lewis never doubted Sue's words nor did he ever learn the truth about what had happened that evening in Teresa's bedroom when Sue had dragged the drunk French lady to her bathroom and hanged her by the neck from the shower head, then let herself out to return, smiling and content, to join him again in the lounge.

Returning home in the plane, Lewis and Sue sat beside each other holding hands. Sue sighed. 'You know something, Lewis?'

'Know what, Sue?'

'That was the most enjoyable honeymoon I ever had, even better that our first one.'

Lewis leaned across and kissed her on the cheek.

'I'm so happy that you enjoyed it, Sue, and that that French woman didn't spoil it for you again.'

Sue smiled.

'No, she certainly didn't spoil it, Lewis, not one wee bit.'

Granny's Betting Slips

Simon Quigley's grandparents, Paddy and Roseanne Quigley, and his great-granny, Rose Campbell, all lived in the same house near the Gasworks on the Lecky Road. Rose, who hardly ever left her chair by the fireside, was a hundred years old. She was Granny Roseanne's mother.

When Simon was seven years old, he visited them often on his way home from school and sometimes Rose talked to him about her husband, Joe, a journeyman plumber. He died of a fever in Ballyshannon, shortly after they were married.

She talked to Simon about her younger days, when society was very straight-laced and when everybody knew their place and how things had changed since then.

'The young ones now are very outgoing and friendly and more open-minded,' she would say, 'but a lot of them have no patience and are spoiled with the modern inventions like the scrubbing board, the wireless, gaslight, cookers and having clean water piped to their back yards. In my young days, we and all the other people living in our area had to get our water from a well at the bottom of a field down the road.'

Simon just sat there blinking and paid no attention to her, for, as far as he was concerned, she was just a doting old woman. *Sure what would a dithering 100-year-old great-granny know about us young people and modern times?* he would say to himself.

Simon's Granny Roseanne, who was about seventy years old and more modern, said that her mother was very old-fashioned and that she never dried up talking about her youth. Simon's granda, who always wore a peaked cap – even in the house – was more modest in his talk. He just sat beside the fire, smoking his pipe and nodding his head in agreement with everything that was said. When Simon went home and told his mother about his two grannies' silly talk and that his granda just sat there saying nothing, she always said, 'Your granda is a very wise man keeping his mouth closed in that house.'

Simon didn't tell his mother everything that went on in his granny's house for fear she wouldn't allow him to visit there anymore. He couldn't tell her about his granny sending him up the street to McGowan's Corner Bar with her brown shopping bag and a note and money, and telling him to go into the snug just inside the bar door. 'Knock on the wee window,' she would say, 'and when Wullie McGowan slides it open, just hand him the money and the note.'

When Simon neared her house on his way back with the shopping bag that held three bottles of stout and a noggin of Irish whiskey, she'd be waiting for him at the door. Taking the bag from him, his granny would then slip into the front parlour-cum-bedroom to hide the merchandise under her mother's bed. She'd then whisper to him, just in case her mother and Simon's mother would find out, 'That's me and your granda's medicine and don't you be telling anybody about it,' while pressing a penny into his hand.

Simon knew that it wasn't medicine of any kind, because he had seen his uncles bringing bottles of the same stuff into his mother's house when they visited his parents. He also saw his uncles and his da drinking the bottles of black stuff along with the strong-smelling stuff that was in wee glasses to make them sing. He always wondered if his granny and granda Quigley, too, would be sitting singing at night in front of the open fire when his older great-granny Campbell went to sleep.

Simon's great-granny went to sleep one night and never woke again. He remembered going to see her laid out in her finery on her deathbed, and her with a little smile on her face as if she were enjoying being the centre of attention. Too suddenly she was gone, and Simon hardly ever thought of her again until his later years.

His grandparents often backed the horses and many's the time they sent him to McCollum's bookies to place their bets. Simon always stood outside the bookies and asked an older person to go in after telling them that the bets were for his granda. Some of the times, Simon's granny would sneak on a bet of her own, unbeknownst to his granda. She told him to back her horses on his way home and to keep the bookie slips separate for her until the next day. When she had a winner, she gave him a couple of pennies to himself.

One day, he placed his granny's bets then went to Meenan Park to play with some of his school pals. They played on the swings and slid down the big banana slide and rode on the shoogly-shoo like daredevils for nearly an hour before he remembered to go home. It wasn't until Simon went to do his homework that evening that he realised he had left his schoolbag behind him in Meenan Park. Simon's father threatened to give him a good hiding and sent him back to look for it. It wasn't in the park and he got a good clip on the ear from his da and sent to bed without any supper. That night, he fell asleep in dread of going into his classroom the next morning to face the master, who would definitely give him more than a clip on the ear for losing his school books and another one to match it for not having any homework done.

Shortly after lunchtime the next day, the class was quiet and, with heads down, they scribbled out essays. During that quiet period, his heart leapt into his throat when he heard his father's voice just outside the classroom door. With his head bent even lower over his writing book, he looked under his brows towards the door to see his da enter with the headmaster. He was called to the front of the classroom. Simon's heart was thumping and drumming in his ears and he felt all eyes upon him as he, red-faced, then followed them out of the door and into the head's office. His schoolbag was sitting on the headmaster's desk and his father caught him by the scruff of his jumper.

'What the hell are you up to, young fellah, getting me and your mother into bother with the school?'

The headmaster told his father to calm down, take a seat and that he would ask Simon the questions. It turned out that someone had found his schoolbag in Meenan Park and had brought it to the school. When the headmaster opened it to see who owned it, he found two of Simon's granny's bookie slips that were just a day old. That was his reason for summoning Simon's father to meet him and to inquire if he knew about his son's gambling.

Simon expected to be murdered and turned into corned beef that day by the headmaster and his father, so he explained how the betting slips came to be there in his schoolbag. To his joy and surprise, they smiled at each other, and Simon got off unscathed.

And by the way, the two fresh dockets were the only things that were beaten in the headmaster's office that day.

Granny Deery's Cat

My eagerly awaited Christmas school holidays had begun as soon as the last school bell rang at three o'clock on a bright, happy winter evening. I was twelve years old and couldn't wait to shake the dust of the Christian Brothers School off my feet. Mickey Rush, my pal who lived next door and who went to Rosemount School, was already in his old clothes of freedom and waiting for me. I soon joined him on the street, wearing mine: tattered jeans, loose jumper and a pair of battered leather boots.

Mickey was going downtown to post Christmas cards and, as we walked along the street, old Granny Deery was standing at her garden gate. We greeted her and asked her if she needed any messages done.

'I don't need any messages today, thanks, but I'm wondering if you wouldn't do me a great favour?'

We said that we would try if we knew what it was.

'My Tom is very ill and I don't think he will get better, for I've tried everything that I know and was advised to do for him, but to no avail.'

I told her that we didn't know a thing about sickness or medicines and that we were both sorry that we couldn't help her.

Then Granny Deery tearfully asked us if we could help her to put Tom into a bag and take him to be put down in the animal shelter. She said she would give us ten shillings between us and would write a message for the animal warden and put it along with ten shillings for him and our ten shillings into a brown envelope.

We realised, thankfully, that Tom was her cat and agreed to do her errand.

Granny Deery told us to hold out the sack so that she could put Tom into it. After a lot of twisting, hissing and scratching from Tom, we managed to tie the neck of the sack with a length of sisal cord.

'Hurry up, now, because the place closes at five o'clock, and I couldn't bear to see my wee Tom suffering for another day.'

That was her final plea as Mickey and I carried the struggling cat in the sack to its executioner in the animal shelter. The tomcat's claws protruded menacingly through the sack until it finally stopped struggling and settled down as we left the estate to carry it past the roundabout at the top of Eastway Road. Our first day off school and we were in the money. What a bit of luck!

'We can go to the pantomime tomorrow evening,' said Mickey. 'And do you know what? I know just how we can make another ten shillings.'

I listened to his clever scheme and agreed that it was a great idea.

Behind the BSR manufacturing factory was a very deep dam known as the Brickfield, once a sandpit but now unused and filled with rainwater to a depth of over 50ft. It was just ten yards away from us, over a hawthorn hedge at the side of the road, and was a very dangerous pond, where many of the local children fished for sticklebacks. There was only one small ledge around the rim, where five children at most could safely stand to fish. The rest of the rim sloped very steeply into the water. In fact, two little children had drowned in it and many children had at different times slipped into the water and were lucky to be pulled out by their friends. The plan was that we would tie a heavy stone onto the sack and throw the lot into the dam where Tom would sink and join the other cats and dogs that had gone before in the same way. Tom was going to be killed by a stranger anyway and *we* might as well get the ten shillings instead of giving it to the Derry Corporation.

When we reached the middle of Eastway Road, we crawled under the barbed wire strung across the small gap in the hawthorn hedge and stood on the edge of the high, sloping rim. Between us, we swung the sack by each holding an end of it. The huge stone we had first tied on to the now-squirming, heaving sack was awkwardly swinging of its own free will in a circle as we counted, one, two, three and away. Down plummeted the stone and the screaming cat fighting for one or all of its nine lives in the bag into the deep pond with two large splashes and immediately sank. We watched for a few seconds, the water calming over again to its mirrored surface.

'An easy-earned ten shillings,' I said.

Mickey replied, a small grin on his lips, 'Aye, and Mrs Deery will be happy to know that her wee pet cat was well looked after by us and, anyhow, what she doesn't know will do her no harm.'

As we crawled back under the barbed wire and returned to Eastway Road, I could feel small pangs of sympathy for Granny Deery's pet cat. I imagined the poor creature's terror as it sank through the murky depths in its sealed sackcloth death chamber to the bottom. Mickey must have been feeling the same as me when he said, 'That wee cat would have suffered a worse fate in the animal shelter where it would have been gassed or battered to death. It might even have been killed by dogs.'

The Christmas cards were duly posted and we dandered about the town before making our way home again up to Creggan Estate. When we were nearing Granny Deery's house, Mickey nudged me with his shoulder and whispered, 'Look who's standing at Deery's door.'

My knees went weak when I saw Granny Deery staring at us, her arms folded across her chest and she as straight as a sentinel. *Did some nosey person watching us at the dam tell her about the cat?*

'Hi, wee Cunningham and Rush, I want to talk to you two.'

We approached her like new-born angels with innocent, childish smiles upon our countenances, my bowels about to erupt. I could just imagine Granny Deery's three big sons battering us.

'Just what did you two do with my Tom? He came back here and him soaking wet.'

Before we could answer, she caught both of our hands and led us into her sitting room. My mouth was dry with fear until I saw Tom sitting there on a big, soft cushion in front of the fire, licking his fur and he as shiny and healthy as a prizewinner and his two eyes sparkling like green emeralds. He must have clawed his way out of the sack to begin a new one of his nine lives.

Mickey was the first to recover from the surprise and told Granny Deery, in his own words, just what we did to her Tom.

'We hadn't the heart to take your wee cat to be put down in the animal shelter, so when we were passing the cathedral, we took him inside to say a wee prayer for him to get better. Then we took him around to the back of the cathedral, still inside the sack, and dipped him into the Holy Water barrel. We felt so sorry for him when we realised he was soaking wet that we opened the sack to take him out and dry him. When we loosened the cord, Tom jumped out of the sack and ran out of the cathedral grounds into Creggan Street. We have been looking for him ever since, and now we are very glad that he didn't get run over by a bus.'

Granny Deery put her arms around Mickey and gave him a big hug; his face went crimson with embarrassment. Then she did the same to me and I groaned as she pressed my face against her snuffy apron.

'It's a miracle and great joy that you brought on my Tom and this house. You two little angels are a credit to your parents and you can keep the money for your kindness and divide it between you.'

We were both overjoyed as she led us out again to her front door.

Going across Dunree Gardens, small flakes of snow began to fall and Mickey and I couldn't stop laughing at our luck. Tom had escaped from the sack and made his way home. Granny Deery credited us for curing her cat and, to top it all, we had earned twenty shillings into the bargain.

When we reached Mickey's house, he frantically searched through his pockets. 'Have you got the money in your pocket?'

A sickly feeling came over me when I recalled seeing Granny Deery putting the money and the message into the sack that was now under 50ft of water in the Brickfield while lucky Tom was now lying contentedly purring on the soft, warm cushion under Granny Deery's Christmas tree.

Ruby's Bloomers

In the late 1940s, Willie Lynch was one of a family who lived in the Black Hut, which stood just a few hundred yards across the border at Killea in the Free State. His father, Albert, soon took them to live in a small farm that straddled the border at the bottom of Holywell Hill, about three miles from where the Creggan Estate is today. Very soon after they left, Johnny Doherty moved into the Black Hut where he later opened a small shop and every Sunday lots of people of all ages from the town walked the road there to do a wee bit of shopping and petty smuggling.

Willie Lynch recalls: 'We got on very well with everyone who passed along the road to shop in Johnny Doherty's and soon made friends with some boys and girls from the newly built Creggan Estate. During those teenage years I spent some of my limited time off from helping my father on the farm by getting up to all sorts of innocent mischief along with the other young country lads, of various religious persuasions, who lived in and around the locality. On winter evenings, one favourite prank was to string lengths of black thread across the road in zigzag fashion and wait until a group of local girls would come down the dark road nervously chatting and giggling until they were tangled up and trapped in our web and then raised a racket by screaming and laughing when we jumped out from behind the bushes.

'I mind one freezing cold night whenever four of us were in Hamilton's big shed with our air rifles; that's where we gathered on many a winter's night to practise shooting pellets at an old bell. One night I said that I was tired shooting at the same old target night after night, and another friend and I went outside to see if there was anything else to shoot at. There was a tight frost outside and every bush and blade of grass was pure white. There were icicles as long as your arm hanging from the shed roof. Well, didn't my friend nudge me as he pointed towards Hamiltons' washing line where Ruby's bloomers were hanging and them as stiff as a board with the frost.

'"What about them bloomers for a target then, Willie?" he whispered and fired a pellet or two at them, but with his gun being so old it had no power and the pellets just bounced off. Then I started to shoot, and, by cripes, within five minutes I'd filled Ruby Hamilton's bloomers with holes. We couldn't tell a soul about it for a long while after; until the hullabaloo had died down about how Ruby Hamilton's bloomers had turned into a sieve overnight!

'We heard some funny smuggling stories then, when things were tight for many people. There was a big woman called Bella who lived in Wapping Lane in the Fountain. She did a bit of nursing across the border in St Johnston and would bring goods back to the North on the train. Bella smuggled the goods in a special pouch she had around her waist.

'As time went on, an alert young Customs man began watching her. He noticed that she didn't look as heavy

195

going across the border as she did coming back. "Begad," he says to himself, "I always thought that that woman was expecting. But now I can see that sometimes she looks fatter coming than going."

'One day, Bella stepped off the train, bulging with eggs and butter. He stopped her and asked her to raise her arms to be searched. Whenever she did so, didn't the heartless skitter of a Customs man clap her about the waist with his big rough hands until the eggs were running down her legs! Then with a big grin on his face he told poor Bella to go on.

'They were happy days then until them ould Troubles came along and ended that friendly, innocent era.'

Aggie Mooney's Bars

Aggie Mooney, the nosey neighbour and local gossip, is coming from evening devotions in St Columba's Long Tower Church. Her first port of call is to her neighbours Cissy and Wullie Daly. She taps on their front door and walks uninvited into the living room where Wullie is slumped in his favourite armchair. Cissy is in the scullery washing up the dishes.

'Yoo hoo, are youse decent?' calls Aggie on entering. 'It's only me droppin in tae swap the bars. Hello, Wullie,' she continues when she eyes him slouched in his armchair.

Wullie raises his eyes to the ceiling in abject surrender when he hears her. 'Hello, beautiful,' he answers insincerely, 'where have you been all my life?'

Aggie adjusts her hat and looks at herself in the mantelpiece mirror.

'You're full of compliments this evenin, Wullie Daly. Are you sick or somethin?'

'I wasn't talking tae you, you silly woman. I was talking tae them two flies flitting around them flowers on the top of that stupid-looking hat on top of your head.'

Aggie looks in exasperation towards Cissy who is

coming in from the scullery and asks, 'Is his head all right, Cissy? He didn't like …' she pauses for a moment, 'fall down the stairs and land on it or somethin?'

'Pay no heed to him, Aggie, sure he's better off raving there than in his bed.'

'I wuz just wonderin if he wasn't feelin well, Cissy, for he looks out of sorts the day.'

Cissy replies in a whisper, 'He's jist in the door in front of you and he has a wee drink in him. He'll doze off in a minute or two.' Changing the subject, she asks, 'Did you hear any bars the day then, Aggie?'

Aggie sits down at the table before answering.

'I'm jist after comin from evenin devotions in the Long Tower and I was talkin to big Tommy Friel and his wife Betty on the way home.'

'It's new-ins for him to be out with Betty,' says Cissy. 'There was a time whenever he wouldn't go out of the door even by himself, niver mind with his wife. He must be getting new life in his old age.'

'Well, he must be changed since then, for he was along with Betty this evenin,' says Aggie. 'Anyway, that's neither here nor there, for he was tellin me that his granny, God rest her soul, remembered the battle at Fox's Corner when she was a wee girl.'

'Imagine that, Aggie, that must have been about a hundred years ago.'

'Isn't there that song about it?' asks Aggie. 'About Paddy Deane hittin Paddy Long over the head with a treacle scone?'

'I used to hear my ma singing it,' answers Cissy. 'How does it go? Oh now I remember.' She begins singing a few lines of the song.

'Holy Moses what a crew
Some of them black and some of them blue
Over the banking they all flew
At the battle of Fox's Corner

Paddy Deane hit Paddy Long
Over the head with a treacle scone
They were at it all night long
At the battle of Fox's Corner.'

Aggie claps her hands in applause. 'Aye, now I remember hearin it before, the song was made up about the battle. And do youse know what else Tommy Friel said? He said that his granny remembers her father got a wile hammerin as well at the battle of Fox's Corner.'

'Isn't that a good wan?' asks Cissy, 'I wonder what they were fighting about?'

'I was wonderin about that as well. I should have asked him about that. But anyway, he said that his granny told him that her father only went out to complain about the noise and wasn't even takin part in the fight and that he got battered for complainin.'

'You're wile naive, Aggie. I don't know why you believe them kind of rare yarns. Do you not think that Tommy Friel was only pulling your leg?'

Aggie looks mildly offended. 'Do you think I'm a gawk or what, that I wouldn't know if someone was geggin me or not? Tommy Friel is a serious man who knows what he's talkin about.'

Feeling apologetic for hurting Aggie's feelings, Cissy says, 'I always thought there was a wee want in that man. His wife Betty has to do everything for him. You must remember his ould uncle, Johnny, who lived near the bottom of Bishop Street? "Johnny Cocoa Hole" the weans used to call him because he kept his tin of cocoa hidden in a hole under a loose floorboard in the living room in case anyone would take some of it.'

'I mind him surely,' answers Aggie. 'And is that who Tommy Friel is, Johnny Cocoa Hole's nephew? I niver knew that.'

'Well, you know it now, Aggie, and that's who Tommy Friel takes after. And as well as that, Betty has him spoiled rotten.'

Aggie is now all excited on hearing these new titbits of scandal and asks, 'Do you think so, Cissy? Do you think he is kind of spoiled or that maybe he isn't the full shillin?'

'Of course he must be spoiled,' answers Cissy. 'Sure he has been tended hand and foot by that wee woman since the day and hour they were married and was always known to sit on his backside from morning to night and wouldn't lift a hand to do anything in the house. The only energy he ever uses is whenever he walks to the bookies at the end of his street and back again. He jist about lifts his feet when she's brushing the floor to let her sweep under his chair. A lazy big brute he is.'

Aggie nods intently in agreement. 'That's the truth, too, for he's one selfish man. He niver lifted a finger to earn a penny for her in his life. Do you not mind the time he bought the greyhound and said he was goin to train it to win every race in the Brandywell and Lifford tracks and make them rich?'

'I well remember that, Aggie, he was full of big ideas that came to nothing.'

Aggie continues her story. 'And soon after he trained it, didn't he sell it for a good lot of money to an English man?'

'Trained it my arse,' answers Cissy. 'He was too lazy to walk the poor animal and it spent its time lying whimpering in his back yard and eating pigs' feet and stale bread. He niver sold it either, for it was Betty who opened the back gate one day for George Hegarty, the coalman, to bring in a bag of slack and the greyhound made its great escape to freedom. Tommy told everybody that he had sold it.'

Aggie is relishing this new titbit. 'I've niver heard that wan before. And I miss very little around here.'

Cissy then begins to tell another yarn about Tommy as Aggie Mooney listens with interest for new bars to spread to her other nosey friends.

'Ah mind one time whenever one of his old pals, Geordie Campbell, died and he told Betty to get a Mass card for him to take to Geordie's wake and for her to write something sympathetic on it for him. She was so fed up writing his bookie slips and doing his bidding for so long that she rebelled and told him to go his own messages and that she was finished being his doormat and that he could get the card himself and to do his own writing; she finally had put her foot down after all those years being his slave.'

Aggie slaps her knee with delight, saying, 'Good for Betty, I niver thought that she would have had the gumption to disobey him. And what did he say to her?'

'He niver opened his beak,' answers Cissy. 'He slinked out the door and got the Mass card himself and had it signed by Father Monagle at the parochial house. He even wrote his own message on it and left it in Geordie's coffin.'

Aggie interrupts her. 'Well, at least that proves he's fully compos mentis and there isn't a wee want in him at all, at all.'

'I'm glad you think so, Aggie. A couple of days after the funeral, whenever one of Geordie's daughters was reading the cards out to the rest of her family, didn't they fall into stitches when she read what was on Tommy's card.'

'What did he write to put them in stitches, Cissy?'

'For goodness sake, Aggie, it would make any grieving family laugh. He wrote: "To my old friend Geordie, Get well soon, Your faithful pal, Tommy."'

Aggie gasps while making the sign of the cross on herself. 'Holy Mother of God, I'll niver listen to that big eejit again.'

Wullie, who has been silently listening, rises from his chair and, without saying a word, lifts his coat from its nail on the back of the door. He directs a grunt of displeasure towards Cissy and Aggie and leaves the room.

Real Cowboys

It's Saturday morning and Cissy Daly, *the wife of* Wullie, *has sent her two schoolboy sons,* Eddie *and* Danny, *to the Gasworks in the Brandywell to get a bag of 'coke' for the fire – this is coal after the gas has been extracted from it; the locals buy it cheaply to burn in their fire grates.* Minnie, Cissy's *spinster sister, lives along with* Cissy *and her family in a small terrace house in Nailor's Row outside Derry's Walls that overlook the Bogside.* Nora *is* Cissy's *only teenage daughter.* Eddie *and* Danny *have come back with the bag of coke on a small homemade handcart that has wheels taken from an old discarded pram. They empty it into the coalhouse and come into the house from the yard.*

Cissy: Youse didn't take long; did somebody give youse a push up Howard Street, then?

Danny: Aye, big Ducksy Carlin was down for a bag, too, and he put his on our cart along with ours and Tillie McGlinchey's and pushed it the whole way home, up Howard Street and down Nailor's Row. You should have seen him, Ma, he's as strong as Ned McDevitt's donkey.

Cissy: God love him, the poor critter, sure he has a heart of corn; I must give him thruppence the next time I see him. Now go you two on out to play and I'll give youse your pay to go to the matinee later.

Aunt Minnie: And whenever youse come back youse can clean your feet on that mat at the front door. I'm going to wash the floor and I don't want to have youse ploutering into this house with your shoes all covered in muck.

Eddie: We're only going out to play cowboys, Aunt Minnie. *She doesn't reply.* You get the guns, Danny, and I'll get wur hats up the stairs.

After a minute or two, they run out carrying two rifles and slam the door behind them.

Aunt Minnie: *Sits deep in thought, looking into the fire and begins to reminisce.* I wish to God, Cissy and Wullie could get wan of them new houses in the Creggan Estate with the electric light in every room, and even an inside toilet and a bath that can be filled with hot running water that's heated by the fire. I heard that there are kitchens that have water piped in to a tap over a sink. Sure they've had it hard enough trying to rear a family in this ould house that we were all reared in as well, and we'll niver get over the sadness of losing wee Seánie last December. Just four years of age he was, sure he was the loveliest wee baby that ever wan could clap an eye on, always laughing and smiling and niver was a bother to nurse, and all the weans adored him. But alas it wasn't to be that he would stay with us on this earth for long, the wee angel, because he was needed more in heaven with all of the other wee angels up there. Cissy's heart niver mended since that morning whenever Wullie came down from the bedroom and told her that wee Seánie was dead.

He said that he lifted him from his cot because he was coughing, to bring him down to the warm living room and he just died in his arms. The wee soul had died from silent pneumonia. Wur hearts are still sore and the weans still waken up during the night crying. *She wipes her nose and eyes with the end of her apron.*

There's no comfort in this ould cold damp house anyway with not even a scullery, and the water tap out in the back yard that you have to thaw out with a lighted newspaper in the winter mornings. And then all the clothes have to be washed on the scrubbing board in the tin bath out in that ould yard every week, hail rain or snow. *She looks down at the backs of her hands.* Sure wur hands are riddled with arthritis with the cold and the scrubbing. I wish there could even be electricity in the house instead of them ould gas mantles that have to be lit whenever it gets dark, and having to run for pennies for the gas meter whenever the light goes out.

Loud knocking at the open front door accompanied by a man's voice arouses Minnie *from her thoughts. It is their neighbour* Paddy Strain.

Paddy: *Calling excitedly.* Are you in there, Cissy? Is there anybody there? Hurry, for frig's sake, before there's an accident.

Aunt Minnie: *Startled, gets to her feet.* Come on in, for God's sake, Paddy, and stop your shouting, you'd think Governor Walker was about to fall down on top of us all.

Cissy: *Hearing the commotion, rushes in from the back yard.* What's all the roaring about?

Paddy: Them two wee boys of yours are playing cowboys and Indians with a bunch of other wee boys on the banking and they're going to get youse all into bother.

Cissy: For God's sake, Paddy, would you calm down and have a bit of sense, are you on the drink again? Did you niver see the weans playing cowboys and Indians before? Sure you play worse games than them whenever you come staggering down the street from Wullie Devine's pub every Friday and Saturday night with your shouting and singing as if you were Josef Locke, and then looking to box all and sundry and saying that you could put Rocky Marciano out in wan round and wakening all the wee weans sleeping in their beds with your antics.

Paddy: *Opens his mouth and stutters a couple of syllables.* But, but …

Aunt Minnie: What are you all in a tizzy about anyway, Paddy, how are wee boys playing games going to get us into trouble? Anybody would think that they were shooting real guns the way you're acting.

Paddy: *Waving his hands in the air.* Listen to me, for frig's sake, your two wee cowboys are riding about the banking on Ned McDevitt's donkey with two real guns and both of them are rifles, and I just hope that there are no real bullets in them for your sakes because there's going to be a few real dead make-believe Indians lying all over the place if there is.

Cissy: Sweet holy Mary and Saint Joseph, where did they get the guns, they must have found them somewhere, for there's no guns that I know of in our house. Are you sure you're not joking or making a mistake, Paddy?

Paddy: I'm not fooling, Cissy, and I'm not mistaken. I was taking my own wee donkey out of the back gate to put it out on the banking to graze whenever they rode past me on McDevitt's donkey yelping and hooting. *He hurries to the door along with* Cissy. Come on, I'll go round with you and bring them back into the house before the police sees them. *They go out leaving* Minnie *wringing her hands and making the sign of the cross on her breast.*

Aunt Minnie: *Kneels in front of the Sacred Heart picture and prays.* Oh, sweet God and his blessed mother, don't let anything bad happen to any of them weans and keep them all safe from harm. *She stands up again and reaches for the brush and continues sweeping the floor erratically to calm her nerves, praying as she does.* Saint Joseph and all the saints in heaven look after them wee boys this day.

Cissy: *Returns with* Eddie *and* Danny. Paddy *is carrying the guns.* Now youse two go over and sit at that table, for my heart's still pounding with the shock. Where did you two get them guns anyway? Your da will kill youse if he hears about this.

Aunt Minnie: Calm down, Cissy. There's nobody going to kill anybody. Wullie doesn't have to know about it if nobody tells him, isn't that right, Paddy?

Paddy: *Nods his head in agreement as he takes the guns to the yard.* I'll push them under the rafters in the coal shed roof and I'll collect them sometime whenever Wullie and the others aren't here. I couldn't take them away now with all them other weans playing about in the street.

Danny: *Calls after* Paddy *who has just gone to the yard.* They weren't stuck in the coalhouse rafters, Paddy; they were wrapped in brown paper in a spud bag whenever we found them at the back of the glory hole under the stairs.

Cissy: *Burying her face in her hands.* Holy God, I don't believe what I'm just after hearing, what would two guns be doing under the stairs and who put them there?

Aunt Minnie: Them ould guns must have belonged to our older brother Eddie who must have hidden them there after the riots in the 1920s, and that's about thirty years ago; sure you know yourself that glory hole's been filled with all kinds of ould clothes and boots and tools for years and was niver cleared out.

Cissy: Aye, I hope you're right, Minnie. I remember him telling us about them times whenever you couldn't even put your head outside the front door in case somebody would have shot you from the ould jail tower or Derry Walls. We were only young girls at the time and didn't even know what was going on; we were that innocent and protected.

Aunt Minnie: I remember my da saying that the local IRA set up a firing post in Saint Columb's College and that they drove the sniper from the jail tower. Our brother Eddie was wan of the volunteers defending the college and he was about eighteen then. I wonder if them guns could have been under the stairs since then?

Cissy: That was long ago, Minnie, it's now that I'm concerned about, but as long as the guns are hid for now, Paddy will take them away tomorrow and hope we hear nothing more about them.

Paddy: *Begins to leave.* That's all right, then, Cissy. Nobody else but us and four other wee boys saw the guns. I'll sort everything out and if anybody outside does ask about them, I'll tell them that they were only imitation ones made out of wood. *He pauses.* Talking about wood, I must leave youse up a bag of blocks for the fire. I have about six bags of them in my shed that our Johnny chopped up from some wood he said he found on the banking last Thursday.

Cissy: Don't be bothering, Paddy, for we have plenty ourselves. My big son Gerry brought three bags in to me on Thursday as well; he said that he helped your Johnny to chop down two of them trees on the Derry Walls. They must be the same blocks, Paddy. He must have been joking, saying they were from the Walls. Thanks for your offer anyway. *Paddy goes out leaving the door ajar.*

The two boys are quietly sitting beside Minnie *on the couch with guilty expressions.*

Cissy: He's a quare good neighbour that Paddy Strain, I must knit him a jumper after Christmas, for the big critter seems to be always wearing that same one for the past year. *Reaching for her purse, she addresses* Danny *and* Eddie. Now, boys, here's your shilling for going for the coke for the fire and tuppence extra so youse can get some sweets for the pictures in Minnie Boyle's wee shop over the back of the Walls. And come straight home after the matinee for I don't want youse to be going up the Derry Walls to get into any mischief whenever the Apprentice Boys are burning Lundy this evening. And anyway, we'll all be burning wur chimneys in the street as well, and I wouldn't want youse to be choked with the smoke. So come straight home and we can all watch the ould traitor burning from outside Paddy Deane's house at the bottom of the street. And remember, don't say wan word to anybody about them guns or about what youse heard in this house the day or youse'll get your da put into jail.

Eddie *and* **Danny:** We won't tell a soul, Ma.

Looking relieved, they leave by the back door.

Cissy: *Sitting on the couch beside her sister* Minnie, *she breathes out a long sigh, then reaches over and clasps* Minnie's *hand.* I'm wile worried about them guns, Minnie, and about our Gerry leaving the house early this morning before any of us was even awake. I hope to God that he's safe and that he hasn't anything to do with them. I'll do no good until he comes home again to find out. I only hope that them ould guns were lying in that cubbyhole forgotten about for years until the day, and that nobody outside hears about them, for you know that when tongues start wagging around here a tiny morsel grows into a feast.

Aunt Minnie: Just you sit there, Cissy, and relax and I'll put on the tae-pot, and we'll get a nice big drop of tae and then I'll help you to finish cleaning the house before Wullie comes in from work.

Nora *enters with a tin of polish and meat from the butchers. She leaves them on the table and is taking off her coat.*

Nora*:* It's very quiet in here, Ma, I thought that my da would have been back from work and that them two wee tortures would have been still running around in their bare feet and their faces not even washed. *She notices* Minnie *pouring the boiled water into the teapot.* Minnie, would you pour me out a cup of that tae, for I'm just dying with the drooth, and you wouldn't mind cutting me a bit of my ma's scone as well for my stomach is rumbling with the hunger.

Aunt Minnie: There's plenty of tae in the pot, Nora. I was just making a sup for me and your ma and I was half expecting you to come back from the town anyway.

Cissy: Is there many in the town, Nora? You didn't happen to see your brother Gerry or any of his friends about? I'm sure if he was working at the quay, he would be coming home on his lunch break before now.

Nora: Naw, Ma, I didn't see him or any of his friends, and everybody else in Derry must be up that town the day. The only person I was talking to was Aggie Mooney, and she said that she would call in to have a chat with you later on in the evening after Lundy was burned; she also said that she had some very important bars to tell you. God, but she's wan nosey woman, she watches and listens to everything that goes on. You have to be very careful what you tell her for she adds bits on to it and she would end up getting you hanged. She talks nonstop at times, so much that you would think that she was vaccinated with a gramophone needle.

Cissy: Aggie isn't the worst of people, and she would do a body a good turn even though she loves the bars and likes to be first with the latest gossip. She's harmless and has a heart of gold. We've known Aggie from we were wee girls going to the Sisters of Mercy School in Artillery Street; we grew up together in this street.

Aunt Minnie: *Stirring the cups and sitting at the table.* Aggie's not a bad soul. Wasn't she a great comfort to your ma and us whenever your Uncle Tom died, and then whenever poor wee Seánie died? She might sound a bit of a nosey poke sometimes, that's wan of her weakest qualities, but she makes up for it with her generosity and soft nature.

Nora: Maybe you're right, Minnie, she's always been good to me anyway. But you have to admit, most of the things she says has to be taken with a pinch of salt. *She carries a cup of tea to her mother who's sitting on the couch.* Minnie *rises from the table and joins them.*

Cissy: *Takes a sip from her cup and addresses* Nora. I have wan other wee message for you to do, Nora, and I think you know what it is.

Nora: Aye, Ma, I've a good idea what it is, sure don't I do the same wee message every Saturday evening to

Barr's pawnshop? I take the ticket and the few shillings from the tae pot on the mantelpiece and go up to Bishop Street and get out me da's suit for Sunday. I mind the time when it didn't take a wrinkle out of me to do that wee message, Ma, but now I feel a bit embarrassed and have to get a good look round me before I go in and whenever I'm coming out again with the parcel.

Cissy: I'm sure you must be, Nora; I was thinking that you were beginning to feel uneasy about it. I should have realised that, because whenever I was your age, I felt the same in case any young men or any of my friends would see me. *She smiles and pleads lightly.* Just go this last time, love, and I'll send Eddie and Danny from next week on.

Aunt Minnie: *Breaking into a fit of laughing.* Do you remember the last time you sent them two up to the pawnshop? You told them it was their uncle's place and they asked if that uncle of theirs was the wan with the three brass balls hanging outside. Cissy *and* Nora *join in the laughter.*

Nora: *Looking slightly embarrassed at what* Minnie *said.* Them two can be wile funny sometimes. Aren't they innocent, too, coming out with something like that? Well, anyhow, that's all right, Ma, I'll run up to Barr's pawnshop whenever I finish this drop of tae, and if you want, I'll call into John McHugh's grocers and square up your tick book. I'll get whatever things you need for the marra on tick as well and tell him to write them into the book for next week.

Cissy: That's great, Nora, sure what would we do without you? McHugh's money is sitting on the mantelpiece as well, but for now we'll just sit here and enjoy wur wee cups of tae, for I think we deserve a bit of luxury now and again.

The three sit in silence with their own thoughts, sipping from their cups. From the street can be heard the children at play chanting their skipping rhymes.

> *On the mountain stands a lady*
> *Who she is I do not know*
> *She has lots of gold and silver*
> *All she wants is Tommy O*
> *Come in, my Tommy O*
> *Till I go out and play.*
>
> *Jelly on the plate*
> *Jelly on the plate*
> *Wibble wobble*
> *Wibble wobble*
> *Jelly on the plate.*
>
> *Sausage in the pan*
> *Sausage in the pan*
> *Turn it over*
> *Turn it over*
> *Sausage in the pan.*
>
> *Burglar in the house*
> *Burglar in the house*
> *Kick him out*
> *Kick him out*
> *Burglar in the house.*

I know a lady
And they call her miss
And all of a sudden
She goes like this:
'Drip, drop
Dropping on the sea
Pull, pull the rope for me
Come, come to the fair
No, no, there's no-one there.'

The Boxer

Wullie *and* Cissy Daly's *family living room in Nailor's Row overlooking the Bogside. Their two young sons,* Danny *and* Eddie, *have arrived home from school and are at the table, cutting and buttering slices of bread.*

Danny: I'm starving wae hunger, Ma. Have we got any red jam?

Eddie: *Wolfing down a bit of dry bread.* Or any syrup, Ma?

Cissy: Here, youse two, don't be eating all of that bread because it's all we have for the morning. God bless us and save us, youse two are always thinking about your bellies and it's wile hard to hould out to youse, for all youse ever think about is eating. *She points towards a cupboard.* Look in the press and bring out them spuds that were left over from the dinner and eat them. And there's still some heels of scone left as well that me and your Aunt Minnie will eat in a wee minute whenever I make wur tae.

Danny: But I don't like coul spuds, Ma.

Eddie: I love them, I'll take yours and you can eat a bit of wur ma's hard scone.

Cissy: Listen, youse two, youse'll jist eat what I give youse and be thankful, for there's a whole lot of wee hungry weans in Africa that hasn't even got water to drink, niver mind coul spuds and hard scone. *She takes the loaf from them before continuing.* And another thing, youse have tae get your clothes ready and do your homeworks yet for school in the morning. So go on now and do what youse are bid before your da comes in and has tae take off his belt to youse.

Danny: Och, all right, Ma, but I like bread and jam better than spuds.

Eddie: So do I, Danny, and do you know what?

Danny: What?

Eddie: I like chicken sandwiches and lemonade even better.

They fetch their schoolbooks and begin doing their homework at the table as they eat.

Cissy: Good boys, make sure youse do them homeworks nice and tidy, and take your time and do them right. I'll get your shoes polished for the morning and get your clothes down from the landing line.

She leaves them alone in the room and goes up the stairs.

Aunt Minnie: *Who has been sitting quietly on the sofa at the fire, saying some prayers.* Pay heed to your mother, boys. We all had a nice day and wouldn't want it spoiled with your da coming home and having to barge at youse.

Aunt Minnie *rises from the sofa and takes the kettle to fill it at the water tap in the back yard, leaving* Eddie *and* Danny *alone in the room doing their homework. Their father enters carrying his coat slung over one shoulder. He is a bit tipsy and unsteady on his feet. The peak of his cap is sitting sideways on his head and his tie is askew.*

Wullie: There's the best two wee men in Derry. Are youse all alone the night, lads? *He throws his coat on the couch and makes sparring jabs with his fists as if he is a boxer, and prances unsteadily towards the two boys, who are staring wide-eyed at him.* Did I ever tell youse about the time I boxed along wae Jimmy 'Spider' Kelly in the Guildhall? We were amateurs wae the Long Tower Boys Club and we were fighting a team from Scotland. *He jabs and ducks and trips over his own feet and falls against the dresser, making the delft rattle.* Shhhhhush! *He looks at the two boys, holding his finger against his mouth. Steadying himself, he takes up the stance again, jabbing and swiping the air.* My man had to get the towel threw in halfway through the second round. He surrendered to my left jabs and uppercuts. I was too good for him. *He stumbles again but regains his footing.* There was nobody to beat me in them days, and I'm still quare and handy with my fists. I was in the army boxing team as well, you know, and beat everything that came up against me.

Jab, jab, jab, he goes, and throws an uppercut that nearly knocks him off balance again.

Eddie: Was that whenever you won all the medals, Da, and was made a general?

Wullie: Aye, son, and that's when I decided to leave the army, for I had done enough of my duty.

Jab, jab, jab, he goes, as he bobs and weaves in the centre of the room.

Aunt Minnie: *Returned from the yard, she is standing inside the back door with the kettle, looking on with her mouth hanging open.* You're back, then, Wullie?

Wullie: Aye, Minnie, I'm making a comeback and raring to go. *He punches the air and crouches like a boxer, again jabbing and bobbing towards the boys.* I was jist telling the weans about the time I boxed along wae the British and Empire Champion, the great Spider Kelly.

He continues jabbing his left hand towards Danny.

Cissy: *On hearing the commotion, comes rushing down from upstairs into the room.* For God's sake, you ould fool, coming home like that, blootered, and scaring the life out of the weans wae your ould bloody nonsense. You couldn't beat your way out of a paper bag, bumming and blowing tae two wee innocent children. *She makes a swipe at him with one of the boys' school jumpers.* Sit down, you ould eejit, and leave them alone. Making a comeback, are ye? You hadn't to come too far back this evening anyway from Willie Mailey's pub in Holywell Street. It's a wonder you were able to make it up Hogg's Folly, the state you're in. It's a bloody disgrace anyway that them publicans are getting away with selling drink on Sundays.

Wullie *slinks to his chair, giving her a sideways glance as he goes. He soon falls asleep.*

Cissy: Now, you two, get on with your schoolwork and not another peep out of youse.

Aunt Minnie *settles the kettle on the cooker and knows from experience when to keep her mouth shut. All is quiet in the room except for the snoring of* Wullie Daly.

The Farland Bank in a Frame
by Joanne Coyle

Feathers frame the Farland,
Clouds are captured in a floating frame.
Beauty pressed in a button,
Lighting in a laundered line of landscape.
Climbing over a wall of wings and water into
photographic freedom,
My camera a keepsake and companion,
A friend of frozen film,
A window into the world.
A swan lake of bright-white ballerinas pirouette past the
pump house.
Raindrops and robins are the prints of the path.
Still sunsets smile,
An honest hologram of the horizon to hold in my
hands and develop at dawn.
Images of Inishowen,
The ivy aerial of Inch Castle.
A picture of paused people and places.
My eyes in an album and life through a lens.

*I have taken the liberty to include this beautiful poem by an
acquaintance of mine from my walks with my camera along
the Farland Bank at Inch Lake in County Donegal. I hope
its striking imagery appeals as much to you as it does to me.*